To my sister, Kathy

DOCTOR WHO
TIMELASH

Based on the BBC television serial by Glen McCoy by
arrangement with the British Broadcasting Corporation

GLEN McCOY

No. 105 in the Doctor Who Library

TARGET

A TARGET BOOK
published by
the Paperback Division of
W. H. ALLEN & CO. PLC

A Target Book
Published in 1986
By the Paperback Division of
W. H. Allen & Co. PLC
44 Hill Street, London W1X 8LB

First published in Great Britain by
W. H. Allen & Co. PLC in 1985

Novelisation and original script copyright © Glen McCoy, 1985
'Doctor Who' series copyright © British Broadcasting
Corporation, 1985

Printed and bound in Great Britain by
Anchor Brendon Ltd, Tiptree, Essex

The BBC producer of *Timelash*
was John Nathan-Turner, the director was Pennant Roberts

ISBN 0 426 20229 5

Contents

1

No Escape

A purple haze glistened upon the conglomeration of pyramids that made up the planet Karfel's principal city. Twin suns warmed the sandy surface, drying any remnants of moisture left over from the crisp chill early morning. Not the most welcoming of climates, and one few of the inhabitants ever enjoyed, the majority living in their special climate-regulated dwellings, which perfected ideal living conditions within large domes of indigenous plant life and fabricated lakes. The outcasts of Karfel escaped the beating rays of solar energy by living deep within the planet's rocky subterrain: huge caverns cut out underground, creating a myriad of passages deep into layers of crystallised rock.

The largest of all the surface structures, towering well above the multi-constructed triangular buildings, was the Central Citadel, a gigantic pyramid that reflected light like a beacon in space. It housed over five hundred Karfelons, including the Maylin himself, his trusted council, the Inner Sanctum, and a crack regiment of Karfelon guardoliers.

There was one other: the supreme power of Karfel, a recluse who enjoyed a contained rule enclosed within a private vault. Only ever appearing on screen, the Borad ruled with a glove of iron, but for some perhaps it was time to throw down this gauntlet...

Tyheer swung the small group of escapees into the shadows as a team of pursuing guardoliers frogmarched past. Gazak, barely sixteen, winced as he nursed his shoulder. The after-effect of the androids' sten blast was taking its toll, agitated by the frantic fight for freedom and, perhaps, life itself. He glanced at Aram, the third member of the group, and offered a half smile, hoping to foster a return gesture of reassurance from the young woman, but there was no time. Another contingent of guardoliers scurried past the sweating rebels with urgency in their brutish footsteps. Clearly the Borad's instructions had been taken seriously, leaving the trio little alternative but to grasp at every chance of realising their liberty. The alternative fate that awaited them was too numbing even to consider. Gazak could only remember the words of a fellow conspirator: *Most depart into the Timelash with a scream.*

It was Tyheer who disturbed Gazak's imaginings, breaking the silence that festered from the disappearing echo of the guardoliers' footsteps.

'We're finished,' he rambled, as two canals of perspiration merged below his quivering lip, following in a thick stream down his neck.

'Not if I can help it,' piped Aram, gritting her teeth and straightening her tunic. 'If just one of us can make it to the rebel encampment –'

It was now evident that Tyheer had lost all interest.

Fear is a strange emotion, preying on individuals in vastly different ways. Gazak, twenty years Tyheer's junior, and already wounded, tightened his stance, leaning forward in Aram's direction. 'I'm with you.'

The young Karfelon woman reached out and clasped the boy's wet cheek, thumbing what looked like a tear to one side as she did so. There was nothing more to be said. A curt nod, more a salute, sent Aram spinning off northward to the Citadel's outer limits, as Gazak turned to reel off in the opposite direction. Within seconds, Tyheer was left alone.

The Doctor's in one of his odder moods, observed Peri under her breath, as she entered the console room. As usual, her companion busied himself around the TARDIS's central column, bantering enthusiastically in an incomprehensive gibberish. A large blue inter-galactic geographia obscured half the controls as the Doctor studied the mass of charted stars and galaxies.

'Andromeda,' beamed the Time Lord, as Peri reached the console.

'Why?'

'Because I haven't been there recently, that's why.'

It seemed a logical enough response. But then Peri was beginning to know her fellow time-traveller very well. Logic was perhaps the last vestige of the Doctor's virtues. She glanced at him, then turned her back to kick her heels around the humming chamber, knowing that this irritating habit would promote a speedy response.

'All right. You win. You choose.'

Peri spun round with a gleam of recognition and

approached the central control console. Silence ensued as the young American girl realised that she had not fully thought out her gripe.

'It's time we put the TARDIS into "park", Doctor. Find somewhere quiet. Have some time to stretch out and relax.' Peri was not sure she was, in fact, getting through to him, so she raised her voice a little. 'We need a *break.*'

For one pregnant second, Peri thought her head was due for decapitation. There was that sparkle in the Time Lord's eyes, the glimmer that could mean anything. All she could be sure of was that he was about to react, and vigorously so.

'So you want a holiday!' he rejoiced, spinning the youngster almost into his arms. 'I know just the place!'

Peri soon became disappointed. The Doctor's enthusiasm for the quiet life seemed predominantly in favour of yet another trip to the Eye of Orion. She cursed his predilection for this planet, even though she had never been there. Yet constant over-exposure had put her off the very idea, and were an intergalactic travel agent to place a stack of brochures into her hands, it was clear she would do all but look at them. It was a simple case of overkill.

Resuming on the Doctor, half-way through his travelogue on Orion, Peri unleashed an unhealthy grunt, one that terminated the Doctor's well-oiled ramblings in mid-sentence.

'Does *nothing* please you?' he barked, returning to the console in a huff. Using his index fingers in an obvious state of dismay he began stabbing at a central section in a way Peri identified only too well.

'What are you doing?'

'Setting the co-ordinates for Earth.'

'Again?'

'1985, to be precise.'

It did not take much more blackmail to bring Peri to a humble penance. Though dissatisfied, she was not about to relinquish her position as personal assistant to perhaps one of the most powerful, not to mention likeable, men in the Universe. Yet there were times when she wondered how he ever built up the latter reputation.

The Doctor removed his fingers from the fine co-ordinate controls, tongue in cheek. The mini-victories scored over his assistant, who was more than a match for his wit and intellect, always pleased him immensely. Sliding across to the other side of the console, he inverted the star chart and continued to study it until his attention was rapidly diverted to a tiny screen near the velocity overide panel. Craning his neck forward, he glared at the culmination of bright flickering lights that glowed more intensely.

Peri sensed her companion's concern through his uneasy body language. It was time they forgot their differences and joined forces. Something was seriously wrong.

Gazak gasped as he tucked himself inside a small niche in the outer limits of the Central Citadel. Realising he was partially visible, the boy scanned the area for some other direction, even though his lungs ached and his shoulder smarted. It was his adolescent frame that kept him going, together with an irrepressible will to survive.

Darting out of his corner, Gazak glanced backwards only to see the silhouette of a guardolier. Releasing a shot of adrenalin deep within his wracked body, the boy spurted off in the opposite direction, but found his path was quickly obscured by another guardolier carrying a neck-loop restraining device.

A final last ditch effort to break free past his captors culminated in a desperate struggle. It took three of the hooded troops to restrain the wriggling young rebel who yelped as his neck was clasped between the iron manacles.

Gazak's flight was over, and the boy's imagination began to work overtime. All he could think of was the Timelash. A black cloud of fear and desolation contained his inner being, attacking every reserve of courage he had left. Meekly, Gazak was led away, the guards quite oblivious to his cries of pain and continuous suffering. The Borad had instilled the 'them or you' principle in all his warriors. Failure simply meant the hunter became the hunted.

Aram could hear the youngster's screams, instinctively knowing her time was also running out. Nevertheless, the Karfelon girl continued to evade her captors until she was faced with an armed android. The awkward mechanical movement of the programmed creature indicated it was about to fire. Aram scrambled her thoughts for desperate inspiration, as the jet black face of the lifeless being, vaguely modelled with humanoid features, lifted its solid metallic arm in her direction. The rebel tumbled forward, anticipating the shot, evading the clockwork mannekin, only to find it re-locating its aim without any warning. With a prayer, she scrambled to her feet, ready to throw herself in another direction, but the grey beam of broken light streaked across the space between them, slicing the air in two. Without any more time or room to manoeuvre, the Karfelon rebel was cut to the ground unmercifully, leaving the android free to carry away his victim like some wholesome hunting trophy.

Deep into the planet's surface, yet not far from the major Karfelon city, Katz and Sezon were regrouping their forces. Up until recently they had acted as two totally independent rebel units, trained and motivated to strike against the Borad's stern reign of terror and control. Now they had united as an attack squad, determined to outwit and restore true democracy. Their new shelter was an old mineral mine that had not been used for at least one hundred years, about the same time as the planet's near demise – a famine so severe that it nearly wiped out the entire population within a year.

Such reflections seemed little comfort to the team of a dozen rebels who had chosen not to bend to the will of the dictator of Karfel. They led simple nomadic existences. Survival was a simple consideration made daily. Possessions, a few personal items, X6 alpha blasters, acquired on a raid of a military supply dump some months ago, plus the basic trimmings of an infantry soldier. The only item in abundance was morale, but Sezon and Katz both knew that even that supply had its limitations.

Sezon was the driving force of the paramilitary

brigade, a tough Karfelon and rapid decision-maker who often placed his life in mortal danger. A stocky individual, with a rugged appearance, Sezon stood for no nonsense, and his hard manner was only tempered by his second-in-command, a resolute Karfelon woman called Katz. Her full name was Katzin Makrif, after Maylin Makrif, the former leader of the Inner Sanctum, who died mysteriously at the time the Borad acquired control through his so-called bloodless coup. Katz was only sixteen then, and very naïve. It took her ten years of servile submission and indignity before she realised what she needed to do. Her fond memories of her father had flourished over the years, as if his spirit had always remained within her, growing with her maturity and leading her to seek vengeance on his part. Katz felt his death was no accident, and she had new evidence that linked the Borad with the Maylin's demise.

Katz and Sezon broke away from their mainstream in order to check a few traps they had set the previous day for small gardinos. These creatures were the only edible animal life on Karfel. Small and bright orange, the hard-shell sand-crawlers offered layers of soft meat when cooked in excess. Sezon relished the idea of having one snared, especially as it was a very long time since the last occasion of such a rare feast. The rebel party were tiring of their staple diet of baked berries and fruit juices.

Winding their way quite apart from the others, the duo, who always worked well as a team, eventually located the animal traps. Unfortunately there was little to show for their efforts: a solitary gorse spray caught up in the main snare. Sezon selected a large rock and hurled

14

it at the traps, causing them to snap shut with a loud clatter. He was naturally upset but more because of general things going wrong for the team of fighters. Katz immediately made light of their bad luck, sitting near the primitive food snares, soon to be joined by her muscular colleague who wiped the sweat from his forehead. The beating rays of the twin suns made life difficult and uncomfortable for their activities most of the time, but their determination to preserve was strong and alive.

Katz flicked sand with the cap of her boot, uncovering a large print firmly embedded in the ground underneath. Sezon caught her chilly reaction, as an uncomfortable realisation grabbed her forcefully.

'Sezon.'

Sezon nodded. He realised too.

'We must have wondered too far west. Didn't think they inhabited this area. No wonder we never caught anything.'

Katz and Sezon were sitting in the centre of a Morlox area. The fact that the Morlox footprints had been covered over clearly pointed to the creatures using that region as a home. The 'corner' technique was a trait of the enormous intelligent animal.

'Don't make any sudden moments,' warned Sezon craning his neck to see if they had any company. 'Maybe if we slip away we'll be all right.'

Both of them took to their feet, eager to leave that vicinity as quickly as possible. Suddenly Katz identified a low moan that could only be a few feet away. She reached for her hand blaster, only to realise that it would have little effect on a fully grown Morlox.

'Let's run for it Katz,' urged Sezon who was in a better position to make an escape. 'You go, I'll follow.'

'Not on your life. We are leaving together – and in one piece.'

Katz appreciated Sezon's loyalty and support, but it was not the time or the place to dwell on such issues. Slowly they both back-stepped, hoping they had not been noticed. A strong aromatic fragrance filled the air. There was now no doubt at all what was behind the rock face a few feet away. The noise of the creature got louder as it now partially lumbered into view. First the long neck, supporting a thick set head and bulging cranium, then two closely-packed eyes and flaring nostrils protruding from the creature's main features, contrasting the large mouth and jagged set of razor sharp teeth.

Katz looked to Sezon for inspiration. Any moment now they would be spotted and an inevitable battle for life would ensue. They held their breath as the Morlox's head and armour-like neck returned into the cave area. Frozen in their places and reluctant to run because of the sound they would create, the two rebels stood their ground, Katz with her eyes half closed in prayer. Sezon, however, decided to take positive evasive action and whispered a command to tactfully withdraw, ignoring the positive risk.

Katz signalled an agreement and they both shuffled away from the area cautiously. An unannounced appearance of the Morlox prompted Sezon to pull Katz into the cover of another cave mouth, and they plunged deeper into the darkened cavern in the hope of not being spotted.

All too soon they realised the cave had no through

route and the Morlox also entered the rocky enclosure, making itself comfortable by the only main entrance. Tucked behind a tiny boulder, Katz and Sezon huddled together, their weapons drawn for some small comfort – but they may as well have had sling shots. The thickness of a Morlox's outer shell meant that only a shoulder-mounted blaster would stand any real chance of hurting the sensitive core of the giant creature.

A howl stimulated their cave companion to its feet once more. To Katz and Sezon's horror, two smaller Morlox entered the tight cavern, identifying themselves quite plainly as part of a family unit. If the three creatures only knew of their hidden guests, they would have inevitably brought forward their evening meal.

Sezon brainstormed his mind for the solution to their unwholesome predicament. Katz was beginning to feel grossly uncomfortable in her cramped position and was acutely aware that their concealment was going to be extremely temporary.

The family of Morlox communicated with each other, gnashing their teeth viciously in play. The cave was filled with a pungent odour, typical of the Morlox. The smell was used to attract prey for food and was the only pleasant feature of the monstrous creature.

A trumpeting sound from outside the cave stopped the family at play as the largest Morlox, probably the mother of the other two, moved out into the open. From Sezon's viewpoint, he could see the Morlox preparing itself for a change of mood and situation. Its tail bounded impatiently and its back flexed aggressively.

Within seconds it had met its match as a fierce battle raged between the female Morlox and the intruding

Morlox. A territorial dispute took shape as the gutteral groans of pain surged between the antagonists. The smaller Morlox took off in panic and fear, allowing their mother to fight alone.

This had to be Katz and Sezon's opportunity to escape and they took it swiftly without any further thought. Running wildly past a ball of matted Morlox flesh – the latest stage of the fight for death – the rebels sprinted out of the forbidden area and into the relative safety of their own environment some five minutes away. Completely out of breath, Sezon embraced Katz. It had been a close thing and they had very nearly lost their battle and become mere fodder for the Morlox.

They made their way back to the camp reluctant to tell others of their adventure for fear of ridicule. Time was moving on and the temperature was dropping. Sezon organised the team and a water system to go through the short night.

Katz flicked her long blonde hair from her face, stirring the embers of a primitive camp fire. The light and warmth below the surface were welcome accoutrements to the resistance fighters who knew the dancing flames served one other purpose. To frighten away the life form that occasionally preferred a carnivorous diet. The Morlox.

Sezon joined Katz, placing his blaster rifle carefully on the ground. Sparks from the fireside reflected along the barrel of the well-kept weapon. Katz poured him a hot drink from a home-made receptacle which he consumed with relish. Each evening they would invariably end up meeting in front of the fire, on some occasions following a burial of a departed freedom fighter. They had agreed to take each day as it came, and never planned more than twenty-four hours ahead.

'Storage tanks?' suggested Sezon, between sips.

'Too risky,' said Katz, stretching out for the first time that day.

'Time we showed them what we're made of.'

'They'd certainly see that, as they collect our bodies.'

Sezon was rattled. He was not used to being challenged, especially by a woman. Inwardly he realised that Katz was not displaying fear, but his body sought conflict, and he needed to release his own hatred and revenge against the regime of the Borad.

'Perhaps if we take a look first? Do a bit of planning. Hit them when they're least expecting it.'

Sezon had to smile at the fresh face of the pretty Karfelon. He admired her pluck, and the fact of *who* she was.

'Okay, but what about the Morlox? We'll have to cut across their territorial caves twice if we don't hit the tanks first time round.'

'Let's just be careful,' concluded Katz, closing her eyes and adjusting her position to make herself more comfortable on the rocky floor of the chilly cavern.

Sezon got up. A sketchy plan for the following day had been made, and it was his turn on guard while Katz slept. He felt the two or three days of facial growth on his gritty face as he signalled all but one of the others to also get some rest, an instruction they did not need repeating. A fairly young group of fighters, once numbering thirty-five in total, they settled themselves for another rest before perhaps their last day of battle.

Sezon took up his weapon and moved to the mouth of

the cavern. He looked into the blackness of the underground tunnel taking up his position between two rocks. There in the emptiness before him appeared an expressionless face as it always did - an old bearded man with sharp Satanic eyes. The Borad.

2

The Time Vortex

Whenever circumstances became challenging, the Doctor seemed to change his attitude and general behaviour, so Peri observed. It annoyed her intensely and often drove her very nearly to the depths of despair.

'Are you going to enlighten me, Doctor?' she bellowed, as the Time Lord flitted from control to control with seemingly little concern for anything else. Then, rather reluctantly, he coyly lifted one bushy eyebrow and allowed his assistant a split second of eye to eye contact.

'It's a blessed Kontron Tunnel,' he mumbled, then resumed his work at the humming controls.

'Then it *is* serious,' snapped Peri, trying to recapture his faint interest in her presence. The Doctor stopped and raised his head. He knew by Peri's tone that it was time to offer more information or suffer the inevitable consequences of eternal nagging, something he could little tolerate, and worked to avoid at all costs.

'In a nutshell, a Kontron Tunnel is a sort of time corridor in space, and we're heading straight for it.'

Hoping this would satisfy his helper's insatiable thirst for knowledge, albeit temporarily, the Doctor dashed to

21

the scanner to observe a dazzling collection of thin yellow bands forming the shape of a cylinder.

'It's there. Just waiting for us. Rats in a trap. The attraction forces are too great . . .'

All this did not alarm Peri, though she did glimpse the Doctor's worried countenance.

'Can't we go past it?' It appeared an obvious suggestion to the young American. 'We are in a time-machine after all.'

The Doctor smiled wryly at Peri's blissful ignorance. 'It's like saying you want to swim to the shore from the centre of a whirlpool. I don't think we have a lot of choice in the matter, young lady.'

A burst of mechanical clatter diverted the Time Lord's attention back to the pulsating control console. As he scanned the delicate banks of temporal instrumentation, a glimmer of realisation crept on to his blank gaze. Peri noticed, and egged him on to share his discovery.

'At least I know where the tunnel originates,' he beamed. '1179 AD – Earth.'

Peri was pleased. It could have been a lot worse. In fact, twelfth-century Earth sounded quite a nice place to stop off and explore.

'Few Americans ever learn about this period in history first hand, Doctor.'

Yet her fellow traveller was soon to put that notion to bed. The Doctor bellowed across the room at his assistant's apparent lack of understanding as to what was about to happen. Simplifying with a curt gesture a gigantic explosion, he left Peri in no doubt as to what could follow.

'And that, my dear Peri, is the most likely outcome of time particles colliding with a multi-dimensional implosion field.'

She squirmed uneasily on the spot, looking for her saviour.

'The interior of the TARDIS will attempt to re-align itself, and as it does so, there will be an internal explosion.'

Peri frowned. 'Is that inevitable?'

The Doctor simply offered a look in the same mould of his rhetorical questions. Peri stepped back. The last thing she wanted to do was stop her companion's work, especially now she knew the gravity of things.

'If you want to help,' shouted the Doctor above the ever-increasing sound of console activity, 'come and monitor these cosmic graphics.' The Time Lord pointed at a small screen to the left of him as he continued working with a bank of levers. Peri needed little prompting as the TARDIS's framework started to vibrate intermittently. She peered at her colleague's face for some comment, but it was quite clear that things were getting a little hot. Even the Doctor could not offer a glib remark.

Aram moved her cheek against the slimy touch of a cold damp floor. It was the first thing she sensed as the pain from the android's shot repeated once more through her small frame, making her leg muscles contract involuntarily until the sensation passed.

Slowly opening her eyes, Aram attempted to focus some attention on her surroundings. The darkness around was punctuated by a collection of multi-coloured lights making up a bank of mechanical controls. The incessant noise of running water emphasised her position deep underground, and her body reacted with a shiver to the cold atmosphere for the first time. Climbing to her feet, Aram clung to the side of the cavern, trying hard to regain her sense of balance.

Announced with the sound of a high-pitched motor, a large mass began to move from out of the shadows into a thin filament of projected light that cast a bright space in the middle of the sodden floor.

'So you nearly got away?'

Aram scrutinised the shape of a high-backed chair, only to hear the occupant's familiar voice once more. It was the Borad.

'You will never betray *me*.'

An injection of fear pumped across the rebel's body, almost capturing control of her voice. Yet with a burst of courage, she yelled to the Borad to show himself. The ruler agreed, and gingerly the mechanical chair began to spin round. Instantaneously, on the point of eye to eye contact, a thick beam of powerful light encapsulated the young girl as she screamed her last. Her wide eyes gazed at her attacker for a split second until they were darkened, and saw no more.

Opening a roundel set into a section of the TARDIS wall, the Doctor continued the struggle to save his time-ship from the Kontron Tunnel. Peri, glued to the screen, occasionally updated him on the situation, though her sketchy knowledge of cosmic graphics left a lot to be desired.

'When I find out who or what is responsible for this time corridor in space...' gasped the Time Lord, desperately attempting to repair a sub-circuit, '...they'll not only have me, but the entire High Council of Gallifrey, to answer to.'

Peri's thoughts were more mundane. With the threat of total obliteration would there be time for the Doctor to avert what seemed increasingly inevitable? She had not bargained on a burial in space, or at least not yet.

'How's the graphics?' bleated the Doctor as he plaited two bare wires together, a screwdriver between his marble-white teeth.

'The curve is now a flat line.' Peri paused for a reaction, but realised she would have to prompt one. 'Is that bad?'

'No,' the Doctor grunted. 'Disastrous.'

The Timelash occupied more than just a central position within the Inner Sanctum chamber. Its pyramid doors opposed the solid giant entrance portals on the other side of the room, emphasising the two ways to take one's leave from the Inner Sanctum.

The chamber consisted of seven thrones, one for each of the Inner Sanctum, and a view-screen that took the place of the Borad himself. Littered about the area were monitoring cameras, commonplace on Karfel. The Borad remained all-knowing and all-seeing at all times.

Kendron and Brunner, two relatively new councillors, occupied positions near the portals, as others entered for the regular daily meeting, dressed in ceremonial togas as befitted High Karfelons. Kendron was a tall individual, though very timid for his stature. He hovered around Brunner, a shorter dark-haired Karfelon, who always appeared more in control of things.

Two more councillors entered, and met at the chamber's geometrical centre, as far as possible from the metallic senses of the Borad. Mykros and Vena were betrothed, a young couple who had found themselves elevated somewhat quickly after former members had met untimely ends, departing through the Timelash. Convicted of treachery, they were dispatched without trial; the way the Borad dealt with all offenders and rebels against his dictatorial regime.

'They're bringing up Tyheer,' whispered Mykros, as he drew close to the lady he loved. Vena was visibly shaken and asked for an explanation. Mykros shrugged, stopping to look over his shoulder. He smiled to some of his colleagues and turned back to Vena.

'The Borad has promised us a better place to live. We must trust him,' she suggested, trying to be objective.

This comment was simply fuel to Mykros's burning fire. A young handsome Karfelon, moulded as a trained warrior, he was committed to peace and democracy, and the time had come to effect positive action against an evil suffocating regime. Mykros took Vena's arms and squeezed her gently.

'What kind of ruler never shows himself? Casts his critics into oblivion and continues to experiment with time itself at the cost of people's freedom?'

Vena reeled, knowing her betrothed to be right, but waiting to stand by her father, the Maylin, and leader of the Inner Sanctum.

'The Borad's working for our ultimate good,' stressed Vena, as she checked her voice and continued in quieter tones. 'We must trust him.'

'And the war?' returned Mykros, as he reminded her of the imminent attack by their neighbours the Bandrils. 'Is that good leadership?'

That was a question that remained unanswered as Vena's father, Maylin Renis, and his personal assistant, Tekker, entered to commence proceedings. Uniformed guardoliers, sporting menacing net hoods that obscured visual familiarity, took their positions within the grey-walled meeting chamber – a dull, matt, lifeless area despite its importance to the planet. But then, most of the Citadel had been downgraded at the Borad's orders. All mirrors and shiny articles had been removed and replaced with tapestries and flora.

As the Inner Sanctum took their seats, Tekker officially announced the Maylin's presence. Unlike his assistant, Renis did not enjoy pomp and ceremony and rarely revelled in his high position. In fact, the stress and pressure of his job was beginning to take its effect on the elderly councillor whose lined face bore evidence of long hours of duty and continuous worry. Tekker, however, made up for Renis's lack of flair in every way. Ambitious, vibrant and highly charged with self-opinionated charm, the pompous Karfelon strutted forward to take a central position.

The meeting took shape with the introduction of Tyheer and Gazak into the chamber. Both men were escorted by guardoliers who used their neck loops more than efficiently on their wincing prisoners. Vena was horrified and attempted to stand, but Mykros quickly held her back.

Struggling, Tyheer unleashed a plea for pity, maintaining his fidelity to the Inner Sanctum and the Borad, though this did little to assist his predicament. Maylin Renis, not relishing the duty he had to perform, stood to read the charges against the captured rebels.

'For organising rebellious acts against our honoured ruler, the Borad, the people of Karfel condemn Gazak and Tyheer to the Timelash.'

Gazak screamed to be heard, despite a sharp increase of pressure about his throat. Moved, but not visibly so, Renis continued: 'Be grateful the Borad has spared your miserable lives.'

With a curt gesture, Kendron and Brunner manned the controls of the Timelash which were situated to one side of the five-foot pyramid's opening doors. Dazzling lights and a blanket of high-intensity haze pushed forward to fill every shadowy crevice in the chamber. Sparkling ringlets of incandescent flares reaching out to oblivion engaged the attention of all in the chamber, generating mixed emotions of fear, wonderment and curiosity.

Guardoliers marched the two condemned prisoners forward to the spinning vortex, as Vena closed her eyes. Mykros seethed with anger, knowing he was helpless to avert young Gazak's fate.

The boy scanned the Timelash, his eyes darting about the room for a means of rapid escape. A last imploring look to Renis merely met with a cold embarrassed turn of the head. Gazak was on his own. With all the energy he could muster, the young rebel flexed his muscles, ramming his elbow in a backwards movement in order to break free. He knew there would be little hope of escape even if he did break from his captor, but Gazak's spirit remained strong, his sense of freedom high up to the last uncomfortable steps of the terrifying vortex.

Struggling wildly, the youth could feel the pain of his shoulder injury sear through his frame like a laser beam cutting through metal. He screamed and continued to contend with the stocky guardoliers who brought all their energies to bear on the kicking prisoner.

Vena pulled a soft cloth from her sleeve and dabbed her eyes. She reflected on her long acquaintance with Gazak and his family. His father had been high councillor of grain production at the time the Borad ordered a cessation of trade. When he still continued to load shipments for the Bandrils, he was taken away from his offices, never more to be seen again. Gazak's mother died at his birth, and so he had depended upon and loved his father very much. His only course of action was to join the rebels and fight for the revenge he passionately strived for.

Now, inches from the entrance of the sparkling whirlpool of time and uncontrolled energy, both guardoliers levered their cargo forward in a thrusting action. Gazak bellowed his last pathetic scream, calling his father's name pitifully. Then, within split seconds, he no longer existed in Karfel's time and space.

Tyheer yelled as he realised it was now his turn. It took four guardoliers to hold his struggling body down before picking him up and marching him to his fate. The chamber echoed with his final pleas, as Renis hurried the guardoliers on. The Maylin was far from happy with any of his sentences, noting the Timelash to be a particularly evil and unnecessary form of punishment. Yet, glimpsing the monitor in the corner of the room, he realised the consequences of failing the Borad's explicit instructions for dealing with insurrection.

Rather like throwing a sack of coal into a burning kiln, the four guardoliers ejected Tyheer unmercifully into the concentric rings of the time corridor. A blood-chilling scream bounced from wall to wall in the room for several seconds after his departure, sending shivers down Vena's spine. Mykros looked at Vena. Any comment would have been unnecessary.

Brunner closed the doors of the Timelash as Kendron shut down the power to the four-sided cone. The dull light source of the chamber resumed as Renis dismissed the congregation.

'What about today's business, Maylin?' questioned Tekker glibly, with a honey-sweet sickly grin.

'Tomorrow,' grunted the Maylin, as he walked to his daughter. Bowing subserviently, Tekker took his leave, adjusting his toga with the dignity of a Maylin himself.

Then, quite unexpectedly, the Borad's personal screen announced a communication. All Karfelons froze to cast their undivided attention to their ruler.

The ageing features of the Borad – a white-haired man – filled the tiny screen. He bellowed a message that underlined the despatch of the two conspirators.

'You see what happens when rebels dare to lift their treacherous fingers against me. I will not tolerate any more infamy. Any further rebellious attacks will be dealt with instantly.' The Borad paused. His small, poker-like eyes burned hot spots on the monitor screen.

His silence was more fearful than his tongue. 'That is all. Only remember I am working for the good of everybody.'

The screen darkened as watching faces broke away from the conditioned attraction of the old man's image. Mykros turned briskly, purposefully placing his back against the TV monitor.

Renis broke the atmosphere and approached his son-in-law to-be. After customary Karfelon pleasantries, Renis tackled the young man's mood but Mykros refused to be led into discussion. Instead he turned the tables on the Maylin.

'Vena tells me Tola is recovering Renis,' he said.

Vena moved forward to also engage into the conversation.

'Tola is recovering as well as to be expected, Mykros. It's all one can expect after such major surgery.' Renis's face indicated his sadness, which the nature of his position forced him to keep at bay.

'I hope you are looking after my only daughter?' the Maylin continued, looking at Vena with a half smile.

Vena herself was far from pleased with matters. The barbaric act of the Timelash disposal was still too fresh in her mind. 'They did not even have a trial, Father.' Renis's expression altered sharply. Unprepared to enter into any further details on the matter, he scolded his daughter for her unloyal protest, taking Mykros aside, his arm about his shoulders.

'You'll have to tame her wicked spirit, Mykros. It's been getting sharper with age. She means well but like her mother she tends to nose into affairs far beyond her comprehension.'

31

Mykros pulled away from him. He glared at the Maylin almost in disgust. It was not necessary for Mykros to qualify his glare, as he was sure Renis understood his feelings.

Without another word, the Maylin slipped out of the now empty chamber. Mykros pulled Vena towards him and they embraced. The camera monitor continued to scan. Deep within the lower levels of the Citadel, the Borad cursed the lovers. Stabbing a button on his chair control, he removed the picture from his view-screen. He had seen enough.

Mykros tugged at Vena. She knew that he was about to risk his own life in an attempt to wipe out the tyranny that constrained them all.

3

Whirlpool

Using a screwdriver to complete the last circuit, the Doctor replaced the roundel and repositioned it within the TARDIS wall. He beamed: 'That should do it.'

Peri was more than delighted, and left her position by the central console, assuming the problem had been solved. Yet her approach received an unfriendly glare from the Time Lord. Peri stopped in her tracks. 'It *is* okay now, isn't it?'

The Doctor huffed. 'We've still got to transcend the time vortex.'

'But we are going to be okay, right?'

The Doctor refused to commit himself to an answer, and marched over to the console and continued working there. He eyed the array of navigational aids and made some adjustments. The TARDIS rattled again as Peri clung on to avoid falling over.

'Go to the store room and bring me the brown leather box.' Knowing her fate if she were to utter a question, she stormed off, quite aggravated by the way the Doctor treated her. The Time Lord smirked as his assistant disappeared. He was quite aware of his attitude, but that was all part of being in control. In any case, he mused,

Peri's fiery temper made for a more interesting day.

Maylin Renis crossed the main corridor to find the steps leading to the Power Vault. Removing the amulet from his neck, he placed it like a key into the main door of the room that controlled all power within the Citadel. Only he had access to this important and vital area, though today his routine visit was to be shared by Mykros, who slipped in as the solid steel doors shut fast behind.

The Maylin turned to see Mykros's fresh young face behind him. He was not pleased.

'Are you aware of the penalties for being here without permission?'

Mykros was silent. He was not about to commit himself that readily. The Maylin's aggressive tone mellowed. 'There are no microphones or cameras in here Mykros; the delta configuration rays harm delicate instrumentation.'

Mykros sighed, quite relieved, and ventured forward with interest. This was his first visit to these vaults.

'I suppose you can stay,' reasoned Renis. 'You can help me.'

Mykros lapped the small room, taking in the nature of the place and making mental notes. 'What do you do here?'

The Maylin knew instinctively he should not answer, but did so all the same. 'I switch power to the Borad's vault.'

'You mean, give him more energy?'

'That's right.'

'That means you can stop it?'

34

Renis was quite taken aback by the very idea, and paused before he replied: 'The Borad'll wipe us out within hours if he sensed any deliberate loss of power.' But trying to reason with Mykros was always an uphill struggle. The young Karfelon mused at the idea as Renis continued to carry out the purpose of his visit. He pulled another amulet from his pocket, similar to his own, but this one had a mirror at its centre.

'A mirror!' marvelled Mykros. 'Haven't seen one of those since I was a boy.' The Maylin was not about to discuss the matter, except to place both amulets into the power panels simultaneously. 'The amulets open the panels to enable me to switch energy.'

Mykros took a closer look. He could read the various sources of energy available, and how the Borad was currently creaming off large amounts of his own vault for personal use. 'No power, no androids, no Timelash, no Borad.'

Renis was unimpressed by Mykros's logic and told him so while glancing at the instructions for the day's power changes. The Maylin's face suddenly dropped, and Mykros was not slow to notice this. 'What's wrong?' he asked. Renis rested his head in one open hand, rubbing his temple. 'He wants me to switch all the power from the hospital today.'

'That's murder!' protested the young Karfelon, shocked by the very idea.

Renis moved forward and began carrying out the instructions as Mykros's strong grip clutched his hand, restraining him from going any further. The Maylin pulled away sharply, and stretched out to effect the power switches as Mykros watched in abortive silence.

'I'll do all I can to support you, but do not ask me to risk my position. Maybe I will have more opportunity as Maylin when the time comes.'

Renis completed the final re-channelling of energy, depleting the hospital of its vital power. With great sadness he ushered Mykros out, only to find an android waiting.

'It's all right, Mykros was simply assisting me,' piped up the Maylin, as he handed over one of the amulets to the mechanised Karfelon. The black-faced creature with short golden hair peered at them with his bright staring eyes.

'Mykros is required in the Inner Sanctum chamber immediately,' chirped the android.

'But –'

'You, Maylin,' it interrupted, 'will attend the Borad at once.'

The Karfelons exchanged glances. Few were ever given an audience with the Borad. Most never returned.

The Doctor dug deep into the leather box and pulled out two sets of straps, handing one pair to Peri. She accepted them with an old-fashioned look.

'Now fasten these around you, and hook yourself up to the console.'

Peri did as she was bid as the Doctor did likewise. The TARDIS engines laboured under the growing strain of negotiating the time corridor in space as the vibrations upon the craft grew worse.

Holding on tightly, the time-travellers underwent the adverse effects of a Kontron Tunnel. Without the belts, both the Doctor and Peri would have without doubt been thrown around the console room and battered severely.

At the same time as they gripped the straps with both hands, the gravitational forces within the TARDIS were removed. The Doctor was the first to fly into mid-air, his feet being pulled to the walls. Peri screamed, never having experienced a ride like this before. She too was tossed into flight, feeling the unpleasant effects of weightlessness.

'Hang on Peri!' shouted the Doctor. Peri's cheeks, now bright red, glowed like hot plates. She gritted her teeth and hung on tightly. The thirty second experience seemed to take forever to come to a quiet conclusion as both travellers landed, making solid contact with the TARDIS floor once more.

They had transcended the vortex, but this was only the beginning.

Maylin Renis re-arranged his toga before entering the vault of the Borad. As he stepped into the darkened chamber with some trepidation, he could feel the hairs on the back of his neck rise to the occasion. As he cautiously entered, the mechanism of the Borad's chair spun its occupant around the chamber's outskirts. Renis peered through the dim shadows, but saw very little.

'Do you take me for a fool?' growled the voice of the Borad provocatively.

Renis trembled, but answered a confident reply. 'No Borad, you know I would never do that.'

'Then why do you plot against me?'

Renis fumbled for a guarded reponse, only to hear his own voice echo about the vault in the form of a recording. It had been stored earlier during the power switching with Mykros. 'But that cannot be,' he reasoned.

'Because there is no monitoring in the power vault?' prompted the Borad. '*Imbecile!* I had one fitted into the dark-centred amulet. When fed into the power panels it is shielded from delta configuration rays.' The laugh of the mature Karfelon suddenly altered drastically to a strong hollow chuckle. Gradually, the Borad's chair moved out into the main light source, as Renis stood and watched the emerging shape – a shape he had never seen before.

Sweating with cold terror, and choking with fright, the Maylin attempted to come to terms with the sight before him. Backing away, he attempted a futile escape, merely falling into the hands of a fiercesome android which propelled the quaking Maylin back into the centre of the vault on his bended knees.

Fingering the arm control panel on his chair, the Borad pushed a lever forward to emit a pure burst of time-energy directly on to his shivering prey. As the Maylin looked up for the last time, the column of white light surged through his doubled body accelerating time itself forward. Maylin Renis aged rapidly to a period far beyond any normal Karfelon lifespan, then further forward until all that remained of him was a skeletal outline that crumbled to dust.

The android surged forward and picked up the amulet from the pile of ashes. The Borad issued explicit instructions to elect a new Maylin. It was time for

It was not long before Tekker had the amulet about his neck and power firmly in his grasp. He adjusted his chain of office before making an entrance into the assembled chamber of the Inner Sanctum. The members present rallied an applause more out of fear than loyalty as the Karfelon's sharp features bid the council to be seated. Vena, quite dismayed by the events before her eyes, rushed to the new Maylin with the obvious question on her quivering lips.

'My dear Vena,' offered Tekker with subtle insincerity, 'your father has suffered a fatal seizure – but the news grows worse...' A curt wave signalled the entrance of two guardoliers bearing Mykros, their prisoner.

Vena, completely shattered and with tears streaming down her face, rushed to embrace the man she loved. From the portals of the Inner Sanctum to the steps of the Timelash, there was but enough time for Mykros to whisper a vital message: 'The strength of the Borad rests in the amulet.'

Tekker, gleefully ordering the time vortex to be prepared, activated Vena into quick motion. She burst forward and ripped the amulet from Tekker's tunic, rushing to the doors of the Timelash to dangle the chain of office just inside. Shocked, Tekker screeched to an android to retrieve the vital key to the planet's power. But in the disorganised flurry that followed both Vena and amulet were inadvertently ejected into the swirling seas of the time-tunnel, leaving all in the chamber numbed by the accident.

Tekker eyed the camera at the far corner of the room. He knew the consequences if the amulet were to remain lost forever. The new Maylin, barely elected, swallowed hard as he sensed the warm flow of blood fill his cheeks, head and neck.

Peri breathed a sigh of relief as she replaced the bracing belts into the brown leather box. A high pitched tone filled the interior of the TARDIS, making her drop the storage unit. She clapped both hands over her ears and winced. The Doctor, evidently less susceptible to the cutting sound, scanned the controls for an answer to this unexpected audio intrusion. And then, at the highest pitch of the shrill noise, the semi-solid form of Vena passed through the console room, as if she were flying through time and space without the constraints of solid matter.

Tekker strutted about the chamber with rather less bravado than before. He had instructed all his scientists to come up with a solution to resolve the problem of the lost amulet, or suffer the consequences. Brunner and Kendron busied themselves at the control of the Timelash, but it was clear that little could be achieved.

'If we don't get the amulet back,' threatened Tekker, 'we're all done for.'

'All five hundred of us?' bleated Kendron. Brunner grunted unhappily and resumed his attention to the Timelash fascia, only to discover a pulsating light being emitted along the vortex's corridor. Tekker spotted the bleeping light too and rushed to monitor the moving entity.

'Must be Vena,' mumbled Kendron, being characteristically negative.

'Rubbish,' snapped Tekker, his confidence quickly returning. 'It's far too large, and travelling in reverse.'

'But what craft can penetrate the Timelash and manoeuvre its way back to this point of origin?'

Tekker grinned enthusiastically. 'The sort that can retrieve the amulet.'

The three councillors continued to watch the progress of the blob on the screen, and it soon appeared as a definite shape. Using a scanner, they were finally able to discover what exactly they were dealing with.

'A TARDIS,' declared Kendron, as Tekker's mind worked overtime. 'I wonder,' he mused. 'Could this be the Doctor's return?'

The Borad, also observing proceedings, was delighted to see the emerging TARDIS, which now materialised inside the Inner Sanctum chamber. He too relished the Time Lord's return, but for other selfish reasons.

4

Return of the Time Lord

Sezon lurched forward, reaching automatically for his blaster. Startled, he turned to see his comrade still fast asleep. Cursing the fact that he too had fallen asleep, the self-made combat soldier stirred the glowing embers of the camp fire. The five hour Karfelon night had passed, and the twin suns of the planet were out in all their wickedly hot glory.

'Sezon,' came a quiet voice from within the cavern. Sezon instantly recognised the half-sleepy tones of Katz who stretched and yawned. The two met by the mouth of the cave for their usual first-light meeting.

'Damn it, Katz, I fell asleep on watch.' Katz half smiled, forgiving the broad-shouldered warrior, but knowing how serious the consequences could have been if guardoliers had paid them a visit unannounced.

'You're just too tired,' said Katz, 'we all are. The life we lead is tearing us apart. We're just not trained for this type of existence.' This did little to soothe Sezon's feelings in the matter and he trudged around the cave, displeased.

'If it were one of the others, I'd have had their hides!' he growled, wishing there was someone else to have his.

Katz built up the fire to cook some breakfast. There was never a lot to eat, a few currants, danjek berries, roasted nuts and hot fruit juice. Much the same as the other two meals of the day. Sticking to military storage targets, the regiment hardly ever got close to raiding food supplies, and all that remained was the sparse vegetation of the planet's steamy surface.

Katz and Sezon were once respected scientists of the Central Citadel, some six solar orbits back. They remembered suffering the rule of the Borad for a similar time until things became too unbearable to continue. Yet the Karfelon was basically a peace-loving being, and it went against the grain to take up arms and fight; the very reason why the majority simply knuckled under the dictator's degrading rule.

At the same time Katz and Sezon decided to rebel, diplomatic relations were severed with their neighbouring planet Bandril. The Borad had broken the Treaty of Co-operation set up a long time back by the historically famous Doctor. The agreement outlined a trade treaty whereby Karfel made regualar exports to Bandril of grain, which was grown and packed in special climate-adjusted domes near the Central Citadel. It was food vital to a planet without the power or expertise to do the same for itself. In fact Bandril's rising population depended on the food supply, and their leaders were very concerned at the break in diplomacy. But until now the Borad still allowed grain to be exported, though the price had quadrupled. Katz realised the time had come for the power crazy ruler's own ends to be satisfied. Much of the payment was in solar power cells, and the Borad had collected enough.

Things gradually deteriorated to a critical level. As trade was halted completely, the Bandrils threatened an all-out attack. Even at this moment a battle fleet was being prepared to enter Karfel's stratosphere. It seemed unbelievable that any ruler would encourage such a destructive move on his own world, but this was exactly the course of events about to take shape.

Katz, still very much a woman despite her torn and frayed battledress, adjusted her hair in a pool of water at the far end of the cave. She used to have a mirror until it was smashed during a fight with guardoliers. Mirrors no longer existed on the planet. A mysterious order from the Borad banned all reflective items and mirrors were the first things to suffer mass destruction.

A scurry of footsteps brought Sezon to attention. He freed the safety release mechanism on his blaster, signalling the others to take cover. Then a hollow whistle indicated the appearance of an ally from the Citadel. Bax, barely an adolescent, jogged into the encampment holding a message tightly in his grasp. He offered it to Sezon, and without a word, took off once more for the Citadel before he was missed.

Katz and some of the others craned their necks over Sezon's shoulder to learn of Tekker's election, and Renis's death.

'More murder.' Sezon threw the paper into the dancing flames. 'Just when we were getting him on our side. What now, Katz? Think you can sweet-talk Tekker?' The group shared a laugh, even though they realised the gravity of the news. Tekker was renowned for his fawning ways, the sort of individual you would treat like a Morlox, a creature you dared not turn your back on.

'Let's make today's strike really count,' rallied Katz, pulling herself together. 'We owe it to Renis.'

Sezon needed little persuasion, and took up his arms. 'Let's hit the fuel depot,' he said firmly, looking directly at his colleagues.

'Across the Morlox swamps?'

'Yes. Anyone object?'

The small group of freedom fighters continued to prepare themselves without a word. Katz and Sezon grinned, and packed away the final items about the steaming fire, doused by water. The group marched out of their resting place and forged their way into the blazing morning sun. The Morlox swamps were a long march away, though getting through them was another matter again.

Tekker unleashed an exaggerated grin in readiness to greet the occupants of the TARDIS, which was now standing in the centre of the Inner Sanctum chamber. His lackeys, Kendron and Brunner, hovered at his tail, babbling to each other about this unexpected development.

'Leave the Doctor to me,' ordered the pompous Maylin, who stood poised to give his best performance as a welcoming host.

'But what if he refuses to help us?' stuttered Kendron nervously. Tekker's lean face rotated purposefully until his stabbing gaze struck its target. The look was enough to send the snivelling Karfelon away several paces, bowing his head to superiority as he back stepped.

Inside the TARDIS, the Doctor had already activated the scanner, and he perused the images with a sparkle of recognition in his eyes.

'I've been here before,' he said delightedly.

Peri was pleased at this statement. There was instant hope of a quick solution to the mysterious time tunnel in space. It was one thing to have a problem to worry over, but quite another to have to worry over the Doctor worrying about the problem. Peri hated it when her companion and friend was perplexed.

'Karfel,' announced the Time Lord gleefully. 'I recognise the architecture and people. No mistake. Last time I was here I sovled their food shortage problem.' The Doctor squinted, his mind in a reverse gear, retrieving thoughts several regenerations back.

'Come on then,' he continued, offering no further explanation, 'but don't go wandering off on your own.' He stressed the last word and waited for Peri to acknowledge the emphasis. She did, but growled her agreement under her breath.

The doors of the TARDIS swung open onto the warm environment of the Inner Sanctum Chamber. Tekker hurried forward with his two assistants marking his every step.

'Welcome, Doctor,' he beamed, with superfluous gestures. The Doctor dug deep into his trouser pockets with a faint smile. He was uneasy about a display of overt friendship at this stage, and allowed Peri to make all the initial small talk, while he evaluated, carefully observed, and made mental notes.

Tekker offered the travellers hospitality, but one matter had to be resolved immediately. The time corridor. Tekker hedged an immediate answer, but offering the Doctor a full explanation in due course, and not wanting to upset the positive atmosphere on offer, the Time Lord nodded his agreement and followed the Karfelons through to a botanical reception lounge, a delight to Peri's floral background. The Doctor eyed the changes around him: an android servant, security cameras, and the lack of light in the rather dim, non-reflective chamber.

'It's changed a bit,' commented the Time Lord, rubbing his index finger along a row of ornate books on display.

'Must keep up with the times, Doctor.' Tekker served up another toothy grimace.

'And why not indeed?'

Peri's attention had been totally captivated by a bank of flourishing plant life near the large bay windows overlooking the desolate planet surface. She revelled in the unusual features of the exceptionally beautiful flowers. Her mind, caught up in detailed examination, was sharply realigned with her surroundings when the android waiter thrust forward to remove the shiny silver St Christopher medallion from about her neck. The sharp tug from the humanoid robot cut into the back of Peri's neck, making her yelp more with surprise than pain. Before the young botanist could object, the creature had made a fast exit rather like some fleeing shoplifter.

Tekker moved quickly to confront his guest offering his sympathy and promising the safe return of the pendant.

'Curious,' said the Doctor. 'Some re-programming is needed for the android.' A signal above the security camera suddenly summoned the Karfelon host into another room. Making polite noises, Tekker whisked out of the chamber leaving the time-travellers to chat. The Doctor had so many questions yet unanswered.

Tekker eyed the interstellar contact screen, regurgitating hateful venom from deep wounds within his stomach.

'What does the Bandril Ambassador want now?' he queried, looking at the limp features of Councillor Kendron.

'Peace,' muttered the assistant, focusing the sharpness of the viewing screen.

Suddenly the reptilian features of a middle-aged Bandril appeared before the two Karfelons. Adorned in the trappings of his diplomatic office, the long-toothed creature, communicating tones of officialdom, conveyed his important message succinctly: 'We do not want war, Tekker.'

He was firmly corrected. '*Maylin* Tekker.'

The Bandril continued. 'Just food which is rightfully ours.'

Tekker spun around, unmoved and disinterested in hearing more from the ambassador of the starving civilisation. He mused at the strong position Karfel had gained since stopping trade with its hungry neighbours. With a smirk, the Maylin gave his final message of non-co-operation, without any possibility of reconciliation for the two planets. Inevitably it meant war, death and mass destruction, but that seemed the last care for Tekker.

As the ambassador of Bandril disappeared from the screen, Kendron squirmed on the spot, fidgeting nervously with his thin chain of office.

'That's provoked an all-out attack,' he muttered.

'Good,' Tekker responded, looking pleased with himself.

Kendron's worried face summed up the horrific idea of a massive intergalactic attack. Tekker returned a hungry look to the councillor. 'Just let them try. The Borad's ready for them, you'll see. His plans will succeed and our planet will grow immeasurably.'

Kendron frowned at Tekker's thirst for power, as he watched the young Maylin glide elatedly out of the room. He bowed his head between his sweaty palms and prayed.

Peri kicked her heels as she examined the contents of the reception chamber. The dull lifeless surroundings did little to inspire her. This was not the place she had hoped to travel to for a relaxing holiday. It lacked charisma – sparkle – and general atmosphere. On top of this, she had to contend with the Doctor's uneasiness – things on Karfel were not what they seemed, especially for a second-time visitor.

She looked at the Doctor attempting to bounce a sudden thought, but the Doctor was already poking his inquisitive nature into every nook in the room.

'It's so dull here,' Peri eventually bleated.

49

'What? Bored already?'

Peri smiled. 'No, I mean dull as in the whole place lacks sparkle. It's all so matt and lifeless.'

The point was instantly fed into the Doctor's hungry mental computer. He churned the idea about, coming to no real conclusion. Yet he had to admit that Peri had a valid point, though he was not going to tell her that. Peri continued to survey the plants in the reception room with interest.

'Ah!' croaked the Time Lord, making his assistant jump ten paces.

'What?'

'I think we've cracked it.'

'Well?' Peri glared at her chief source of inspiration only to get a limited response. Footsteps could be heard and Tekker's return prompted the Doctor to revert to his passive saunter, both hands firmly clasped behind his back.

The Maylin darted back into the room as swiftly as he had departed, beating a path to the Doctor and attracting the Time Lord's undivided attention. An enigmatic glint sparked across his prying eyes as if he were desperate to engage in mind games with the famous time-traveller. Offering Peri the chance to explore the plant life that littered the Citadel's extensive network of corridors, Tekker dangled a metaphorical carrot before the Doctor, tempting him to learn more about the Timelash – the massive time vortex in space. Peri listed a string of good reasons why she ought not to leave her companion, but stood little chance of being taken seriously after the Doctor himself fully agreed she should take her guided tour. And that was that.

Councillor Brunner escorted the young visitor out of the chamber and around the Citadel complex while other business was discussed behind closed doors.

A concealed guardolier primed his neck-loop standing in readiness to act on command. He squinted at Peri as she sauntered past with Brunner, his fingers eager to operate the device he was fully trained to use.

'Beautiful flora,' said Peri, trying hard to be polite as well as conversational.

'From Bandril,' returned Brunner, quickly giving her a potted background on the flowering shrub under her gentle touch. 'Mind the next one,' Brunner warned, telling his guest of the dangers of the violet-striped flower that emitted a steam of acidic juice when agitated. Peri stuck her tongue out at the plant as Brunner led the way forward. She was not enjoying her trip at all, all too eager to be back at the Doctor's side.

Brunner's communicator summoned the councillor away, leaving Peri to wander on her own. She paced a long corridor that led to a large door with a central locking device. Not wishing to pursue that direction, she turned to see the giant features of a guardolier in full uniform facing her. Timid, she smiled at the veiled soldier, but there was no response. Instead the Karfel warrior opened the clasp of the neck-loop harness, pointing the awesome instrument in Peri's direction. Further menacing movements led her to commence a hurried retreat, but despite calls for help, she was now very much on her own, facing the first of many major challenges on this dangerous planet.

5

Negotiating the Timelash

Peri managed to escape the Citadel before the fire of an android, who had joined in the pursuit, hit its intended target. Closing the heavy hatchway behind her, which led on to the planet's dry surface, she scrambled clear of the massive pyramid structure and darted into a rocky area with plenty of cover.

She stopped to catch her breath, gazing up at the view of a crimson skyline. The giant fireballs of Rearbus and Selynx, Karfel's twin suns beat down an acrid heat on Peri's sweating forehead. She could feel her pulse race to keep her frightened body functioning as her spirit regained composure despite her unpredictable future. Peri cursed her luck, quite annoyed at the Doctor's irresponsible and fickle act of 'off-loading' her merely to accelerate his thirst for knowledge of the Timelash.

Glancing around, there seemed little point in deliberating any further. Action was required, but there was not a lot to choose from. Northward lay sand; south, more sand and gorse bush vegetation; east, the Citadel, and west, more rocks and caves. Perspiring more than ever, she put on a brave face and trudged in the direction of the caves. Perhaps some shade would revive her before she decided her next move in the parched inhospitable environment.

Brunner questioned the android as they scanned the horizon for their lost guest.

'Nothing that way but sand, thirst and Morlox,' he reasoned, allowing the android to firmly close the sealing hatch once more. 'Those creatures'll make a meal of her soon enough. Either way she's finished, poor child.'

The councillor took his leave, allowing the android to continue its way to the lower vaults in order to make a report to the Borad. Brunner had other matters to attend to, none of which he relished. Mainly this concerned an explanation of Peri's disappearance to Tekker, but he would think of something.

The search for Peri was on. Guardoliers were called up in large numbers and scattered throughout the Citadel. The Borad was angered at the girl's escape and Tekker knew his delicate, if not dangerous, position. He had to locate her and fast, passing the buck to his troops and helpers. An emergency Council meeting was called and heads of departments summoned. For some reason, Peri's importance had been overlooked and now she was searched for with all the vigour of a major rebel hunt and more. An exterior search unit was assembled before Tekker himself. The lean, hungry-looking Maylin stared at each member of the six-strong unit which stood rigidly to attention.

'I want that girl alive,' seethed Tekker. 'If you dare come back empty-handed it will mean a Timelash execution for each and everyone of you.'

Tekker paused to check he had instilled sufficient fear into the souls of the guardoliers before him. 'Is that understood?' The group howled their understanding and obedience before being dismissed, leaving Tekker to move on and stimulate others into action with equal threats. Most important of all, he had to ensure the safety and future of his own neck.

Peri scrambled along a sharp rock face which led to a narrow escarpment, giving her enough room to stop and inhale deeply. At the back of her mind lurked the chilling features of the pursuing android and, even knowing she had evaded this hunter, Peri still continued to glimpse over her shoulder all the same. She felt sticky and uncomfortable, wondering how a reunion with the Doctor could be organised. The inhospitable atmosphere and rugged terrain surrounding did little to boost a flagging morale.

Then the young traveller sensed a strange fragrance. The smell increased, forcing Peri to investigate the source of the rich aroma. Moving off the narrow ledge, she crawled into a confined space, a small cavern eaten out of the rocks by water over hundreds of years. There in the half-light a long rounded boulder invited Peri to stretch out and relax. She did so, parking herself squarely on the wedge of compact stone. Lifting up her legs, she threw her head and shoulders back, enjoying the cold feel of the icy rock, protected from the incessant rays of the twin suns.

In the quiet of this unguarded moment, Peri effected a casual gaze about her. Then the rock beneath trembled as if monitoring an impending earthquake. She jumped to her feet and watched the granite mass elevate slowly, taking on the shape of a gross vile-headed beast. Two bright eye sockets completed the visage of this bizarre creature as its craterous mouth slid open to reveal yellow cracked teeth as sharp as any knife. It salivated with thick green spittle.

Albeit somewhat delayed, Peri unleashed an almighty scream, reeling back into the cave's darker corner. But the truth of the matter remained – the monstrosity was eager to get its prey and there was nowhere to run.

The Doctor paced the reception room quite rattled by Tekker's irritating grin.

'You expect me to believe this preposterous story?' yelled the Time Lord, puckering his mouth in disgust. 'That a lady of the Inner Sanctum just happened to fall into the time vortex with a vitally important key to your planet's power?'

Tekker responded to the Doctor's high-handedness with exaggerated pomposity. He rose to his feet and delivered a look of extreme annoyance and impatience.

'Yes, Doctor,' he eventually concluded. 'And there's little time left for you to retrieve it.'

The Doctor could not believe his ears, and stormed over to meet the Maylin almost nose to nose. 'And give me one good reason why I should!' he demanded emphatically.

Tekker returned his cheeky look with a blend of one-upmanship. 'Peri,' he laughed, watching his guest's face fall.

Peri screamed, clutching the slimy wall of the tight cave as the long gnashing snout of a large Morlox trapped her in an inescapable position. Enormous fangs protruded from the bellowing creature, as it threatened Peri's very existence. It sized up the prey before its bright bulging eyes and moved closer, ready to snatch a first bite.

'Fire!' a distant voice commanded as a burst of blaster-fire hit the elongated neck of the tunnel monstrosity, making the lumbering animal yelp and back off from its intended meal. Peri flicked her head to one side relieved by the retreat of the creature.

Four troopers headed by Katz and Sezon continued fire until they had forced the Morlox back into the murky black depths of the caves. Katz dashed forward to move Peri away, but suddenly a burning android that materialised somehow from nowhere blocked their path completely.

Sezon signalled the others to butt the smouldering remains and make a path of escape. Peri did not argue or ask questions and clung to Katz making a clean hurried exit.

The attack force led by Sezon headed for cover some way from the dangerous tunnels renowned for Morlox. Katz hustled Peri to one side as the task force unit regrouped in the cover of some scattered rocks. Sezon stared at the unknown girl with suspicion, ordering the team to stay on watch at all times.

56

'Who is she?' quizzed the commander. Peri opened her mouth to answer but was given little opportunity to respond.

Katz piped up, snapping a curt reply: 'She's not one of ours.' Sezon pronounced instant judgement on the young girl, sentencing her life to be terminated at once. Peri was confused, not sure whether she could believe her ears. There seemed little point in being rescued only to find her fate sealed yet again.

'Wait, I'm not a spy,' she insisted, looking imploringly at Katz who was more her age. 'Please, you've got to believe me.'

Something in Peri's tone made Katz interested in hearing more, even though Sezon goaded her on to carry out his sentence of execution upon the suspected spy from the Citadel. Peri begged to be given a chance to prove her innocence, but the impatient rebel leader preferred simply to carry on their day's strike without having to drag dead wood with them.

'I said, kill her!' Sezon was losing his temper now. 'She's bound to be one of the Borad's lackeys. Come on, we're wasting time.'

The vault of the Borad was buried deep within the Citadel. This nerve centre drained large reserves of power, in order to convert pure energy to activate the many time experiments conducted by Karfel's tyrannical ruler. His insatiable obsession with time continued to feature as an all-consuming passion. No one quite knew what exactly he was searching for, though many had experienced the 'side' discoveries he had already made. One such find was the Timelash: a temporal corridor spanning centuries and galaxies through the universe.

The Borad moved along his control banks, gliding to a halt in his high-backed chair. The motors were charged to contend with a heavy weight. Despite his light framed appearance on Karfel viewing screens, the Borad remained a bulky mass that could not support itself any longer. Androids offered the ruler individual attention, and were programmed to guard and protect the being that had stolen the freedom and liberty of a once peace-loving society.

Lifting his stocky black gloved hand, the ruler activated a replay tape on which was recorded Peri's image. The Borad closely observed the young attractive outline of the Time Lord's assistant with relish.

'A plucky creature who knows how to look after herself,' he said, thinking out loud. 'I have a use for this pretty little time-traveller. If she's still alive, bring her to me.'

The nearest android registered its agreement to the order and made mechanical movements to the sealing doors so as to carry out the request. The Borad continued to observe a still picture of Peri. He was becoming more and more infatuated with this vision of loveliness.

'I have long been waiting for someone as lovely as you, my dear.'

The Doctor's brain buzzed as he considered possible solutions to the predicament before him. Should he leave Peri in search of a lost lady of the Council and her amulet? Or refuse Tekker's demands, calling his bluff? Essentially his young assitant's safety was of paramount importance, and he owed it to her not to forget.

'Blast you, Tekker,' grunted the Doctor in dismay. 'What have you done with Peri?' Tekker gleamed as the Time Lord continued. 'When I was last in nineteenth-century America I learned the term 'Mexican Stand Off'. On Orion it's called a 'double-edged matrix marker', and on Karfel...'

'On Karfel, Doctor,' interrupted Tekker, 'you call it power to the one holding the trump card. Admit defeat. Go on, you've got everything to lose by not following my simple request.'

'Simple,' muttered the Doctor. 'Simple!' he shouted above Tekker's voice. There was a pregnant pause. 'Simple!!' the Doctor bellowed loudly across the echoing room.

An android edged forward, making its presence known, raising an arm as if to threaten.

'Time to go, Doctor,' rolled Tekker glibly as he pointed in the direction of the TARDIS. 'Pleasant journey.'

Knowing there was little choice in the matter, the Doctor reluctantly opened the TARDIS door. Tekker waved gleefully, realising he had won his first tussle with the famous Doctor. The Doctor himself bit his tongue in an effort not to lose control of his cool exterior even though he was burning with a white hot rage within. A final look at Tekker sent the Time Lord inside the TARDIS, operating the door mechanism with a flick of annoyance.

'Just wait till I get back, Tekker,' muttered the Doctor to himself. He stood before the centre console and glared at the levers in his reach. Clearly he knew what he had to do, but the idea of leaving Peri, even for a modicum of time, played heavily on his conscience. He had to make some effort to trace her, but how?

A sudden flash of inspiration reminded him of Karfelon body temperature. It was 37.6 celsius, somewhat lower than his hot-blooded assistant. If he could just scan the area around the Citadel, maybe he could pinpoint her whereabouts and simply rematerialise to pilot a rescue.

Engaging the necessary circuits, the Doctor decided to put his plan into action. His searching eyes scanned the oval tracker screen intently. Myriad dots of life slowly emerged from the darkness of the rotund glass. Adjusting the appartus finely, the Doctor hoped to pick out just one brighter than all the others, but even the optimistic Time Lord soon realised his task was going to be too tough.

'Come on Peri, show yourself. You're here somewhere, I know you are.'

Sezon paced the area around Peri who was now securely manacled.

'Who are you?' he growled, in an unfriendly manner.

Katz looked on, watching the captured 'guest' react to the bombardment of interrogation.

'Are you a spy for the Borad?'

Peri pulled forward from her bindings. 'Who?'

'Don't mess with us.' The rebel leader placed his

hand blaster against her perspiring cheek. 'Or you know what'll happen.'

Peri, quite scared now, appealed to Katz with a look of desperation. The response was positive and Katz instinctively knew Peri was not guilty of espionage.

'Come on, you must tell us,' she said imploringly. 'I'm patient, but my colleague Sezon's less tolerant.'

Peri squirmed and looked up again at the deadly barrel of the sonic blaster.

'He means it, you know.'

Sezon released the safety catch.

'Okay, okay,' Peri directed her voice to Katz. 'But you'll never believe me.'

Katz frowned. 'Try me.'

Peri didn't know where to begin, but taking a deep breath, exhaled her story.

'I travelled here with the Doctor –'

Sezon grunted and immediately interrupted her flow. 'You must take us for fools. Next you'll be talking of the TARDIS.'

'But that's right,' she nodded, looking to Katz for some sign of support. Sezon, however, pushed the nozzle of the blaster between Peri's eyes. 'Five seconds,' he uttered.

Katz tossed the weapon to one side, rattled by her colleague's eagerness to indulge in more violence.

'There's another way. I have an idea.'

The Doctor cursed his luck and shut down his thermal search circuit with one stroke of his right index finger. The lights on the unit diminished until there was a jet black screen once more.

The co-ordinates were now set for the ultimate destination of the Timelash, Earth, though the Doctor had reasoned there would be a time deflection co-efficient to take into account, due to Vena transcending the vortex through the TARDIS. A date was then entered into the ship's computers and a course was set for Victorian England.

Katz fumbled in her tunic and retrieved a small silver locket which she gingerly opened in front of Peri's wide-eyed stare.

'The pendant was given to my father by the Doctor's assistant on her visit to Karfel. If you are who you say you are, you should know her name.'

Peri glanced at the small photograph and lock of hair inside the locket. She grimaced, wracking her brains to remember the girl's face.

'The Doctor had so many assistants. I can't remember them all.'

Sezon repositioned his blaster.

'Wait!' Peri yelled. 'I'm thinking. Give me a chance!'

A pregnant pause ignited the vague name in her mind. Gradually the word took shape until it reached the tip of her tongue, and was promptly spat out, just in the nick of time.

'Jo! Jo Grant!'

Katz puffed, relieved, almost as if it were *her* life that had been threatened. Turning to Sezon, she flashed him a single admonishing look which signified her feelings in the matter.

Katz freed Peri in state of glee. Not only had she prevented a further display of violence, a necessary but loathsome evil in her mind, but she had gained a special friend, one who knew the Doctor personally.

Peri asked the obvious about their connections with her mentor.

'My father and the Doctor were very good friends, Peri. They spent many happy hours together when he was last on Karfel.' Katz went on to explain how the Doctor had saved the planet from starvation by inventing a technique to manufacture grain artificially in large quantities. This was something quite incredible on a planet with few resources and endless waste areas. 'The technique was very successful,' Katz continued, 'and Karfel flourished. For a time everything went extremely well, but when the Doctor left us, there was a change in government. My father, the Maylin, was murdered.' Even though Katz had recounted the story many times, she had to stop to regain her composure. Sezon stepped forward to comfort her but she waved him back. 'I'm all right.' Bidding Peri to sit with them, she continued her account. 'Of course I can't prove it, but it all adds up.' Peri's view of Karfel was now taking shape for the worst which only made her fret more for the safety of the Doctor.

'The Borad killed my father as he took power by force,' continued Katz. 'The violence he used ensured that no one dared attempt to stop him. It was awful.'

Sezon offered Peri a drink in a manner which stressed his apologetic mood. Peri accepted it cheerfully. Looking around her surroundings, Peri could see that the other rebels in the group were all very young, though Sezon explained that many of them had rapidly aged in the short space of time they had been away from the Central Citadel. The harsh climatic conditions, rougher existence and physically demanding way of life took its toll unmercifully on the freedom fighters. Some of them had been technicians and scholars not used to violence and revolt, yet all of them without exception had lost someone close to them through the ruthless rule of the unseen Borad. It was a melancholy group that Peri felt deeply for, especially since they had rescued her from the clutches of the cave creature.

Katz arranged as many comforts as could be offered to their new guest, as Sezon showed his warmer side. It was good for the group to meet with a new face and a different topic of conversation. Indeed, Earth became a major topic which took up most of the evening.

The Doctor renegotiated the unstable time corridor once more, making his way through time and space to a planet he had visited on many occasions. This time however he knew his stay would be brief. There was so much he had to return to do on Karfel.

The Doctor never really knew why he had a soft spot for the planet Earth. Unknown to anyone else, he had a pre-programmed circuit that automatically took up course and headed for the planet with the flick of a tiny lever. Yet the Time Lord always insisted he had laboriously to set his controls each time. He mused at his harmless deceit, reflecting on the many friends he had made and lost over the centuries of the planet's rich history through which he had travelled. From the time of his very first visit to the planet he had become besotted and emotionally attached to the people – some more eccentric than himself – and the rich wealth of challenge and experience that the planet offered adventurous time-travellers.

But the Doctor's priorities were clear. He had to locate Vena and return the amulet, or at least be in a position to negotiate with Tekker and the Borad. He pondered at the many ways he could return to Karfel – with a crack unit of British assault troops for example, or locate his Samurai friends in early Japenese history. But that would be cheating and the Time Lord contented himself to resort to his inner powers in order to fight and win.

The TARDIS broke through the time vortex eventually, darting into the time-space of Earth's nineteenth century. Heading for Europe, the Doctor allowed the TARDIS to be propelled by the final diminishing forces of the corridor to its resting place, Scotland. The Doctor was eager to leave and begin his search. He did not relish the thought of scanning mountains and lochs in the process, but he had little choice in the matter. The thought of Peri in detention, or worse, forced him to accept his predicament and make the most of it.

A quick scan of where he was, indicated a decided lack of life. But for a tiny cottage there was little else around and certainly no sign of Vena. The Time Lord prayed his calculations were correct. Being a week, or even a day out, would be disastrous. The search for Vena and the amulet was on.

6

Stirring Embers

The cottage was quite a cosy place really, despite it not being used for most of the year, but then Herbert always took a great delight to make it that way before getting down to any serious writing – or fishing. It all rather depended on how the mood took him. Though not especially tall, he was a well-built young man in his early twenties. Always well-attired, he had an eye for the ladies, a trait he never concealed.

Herbert entered the cabin after a morning's fishing. He removed his wet wellington boots and padded in his socks to the log fire to stir the dying embers. It was his sixth day in Scotland, and he loved the fresh atmosphere around the loch. Yet his thoughts would often wander from his writing to ideas beyond the stars themselves.

Not far from the fireplace, there stood a rickety mahogany table. Upon its highly polished surface were the letters of the alphabet neatly arranged in a circle. In the centre of the spread of letter cards was an upturned wine glass and on the floor near the table lay a large black book, its cover embossed with the design of unusual symbols and figures as befitting a witch or necromancer.

Herbert eyed the book and table. There was a glimmer of temptation in his blue eyes. Dare he work further on his project? Bouncing up from his seat, the fire behind him now crackling, Herbert dipped into the somewhat dusty manual. He thumbed through its pages searching for a section that he had already read previously, entitled 'Calling Up The Spirit Of The Glass'.

Closing his eyes tightly, he memorised a passage that had already been scored and marked heavily. Slowly he opened his eyes and dispensed with the book of magic, sitting himself comfortably at the small table. He placed his left index finger on the upturned glass. A cold shiver ran down his spine, and his torso shook momentarily, as an unusually strong atmosphere seemed to present itself in the room. Herbert began to feel a little cold though the fire had now got well under way, and he bunched his toes together, rubbing his feet at the same time.

Although it was two o'clock in the afternoon the lighting in the room seemed to dim, despite the brilliant May sunshine outside. Herbert sensed he should move the glass, and as he did so, the wine goblet began pushing his fingers vigorously from letter to letter. He shivered at this uncanny development to contact the other side. Then, culminating with a spray of sparks in the fireplace, the glass spun violently from the table, smashing into several pieces on the stone floor by the doorway. Before Herbert could react, a spiralling column of air swept the cards and table to opposite sides of the room. Books, candleholders, loose furniture, fixtures and fittings were scattered mercilessly about the room. Herbert found himself thrust tightly into a corner unable to counter the unseen force in the room.

Gradually a white outline emerged from the chaos. Herbert dived for the crucifix and swung it around his neck for protection. The ghostly shape of Vena materialised before Herbert. Glimpsing his timid face, she collapsed and fell on the stone floor.

Sezon drew up a large rock in front of the camp fire. The contrasting cold evenings on Karfel always required plenty of artificial heat. He offered the make-do seat to Peri, who was still getting used to the fact that he was on her side.

Katz took the opportunity to discuss the state of affairs on Karfel as they currently stood. 'Which ruler would actually want to provoke an all-out attack on his own planet?' she asked, as Peri listened with concern.

'What would he achieve, killing everyone on this planet?' returned Peri, mystified.

'Not everyone.' Sezon moved nearer the welcoming heat of the camp fire. 'The Bandrils have a bendalypse warhead which they won't hesitate to use. It'll completely annihilate all life here that supports a central nervous system.'

Katz stoked the fire. 'Except the Morlox – they don't have one.'

'Would sort of make him king of the desolation,' concluded Peri.

Katz smiled and stretched out to relax for the night as Sezon checked the guard detachment. Peri looked into the bouncing flames. She wondered about the Doctor, but had little chance to expand her thoughts.

There was a scuffle at the main entrance to the cave. Instantly Sezon rolled over to load his blaster only to find the cavern overrun with Citadel guardoliers. Katz looked up from her place on the ground. She could see Sezon's expression of horror and despair as all the rebels were herded together in a corner of the encampment. Their future looked bleak, as Katz above all realised, only being able to offer a smile of apology to Peri who appreciated the friendly gesture.

Herbert, nodding off, slipped his elbow on the mahogany table and jolted sharply. He checked the lady who had presumably been summoned and who was now sleeping soundly on the couch. He reached forward to touch her, afraid she would evaporate as quickly as she had materialised. Herbert stroked her fine brown hair, and retracted his hand as soon as the woman stirred. Vena opened her pretty eyes and sat bolt upright with a start. She snaked her head around to evaluate her location eventually allowing her gaze to rest on the fine handsome features of her host.

'Where am I?' she queried. 'And where's my –'

Herbert pre-empted her. 'The talisman's under your pillow.'

Vena rummaged around the bedclothes for the amulet, clutching it like a lifeline. 'They must not get it,' she said. Fear was written indelibly over her face.

Herbert noticed her to be a typical lady in distress. He dwelled on the idea and pandered to the notion.

'I'm Vena. Thank you for looking after me,' she said.

'The pleasure's all mine, dear lady.' Herbert, typical

of his generation, underlined his politeness and common decency. 'Though I assume you're from up there' – he pointed heavenwards – 'rather than down there.'

Vena grinned. She liked his simple direct manner. 'You could say, I'm from beyond the stars.'

The young Victorian man performed a mental somersault. 'Fantastical!' he declared, edging forward to learn more from his mysterious visitor from the stars.

'But what about you? Tell me, please?' Vena's soft gentle approach ignited a spark within Herbert's inner being. It was not long before an explanation about his holidays in Scotland was forthcoming, and that he was a teacher about to start school next term.

The conversational patter was eventually dissected by the drone of the TARDIS's engines. The couple, assuming the worst, scurried around the room. Vena hid the amulet as her host flicked through his manual of magic to the page that read 'Ridding Unwanted Spirits'.

The Doctor opened the TARDIS doors to greet the splendid sight of the Scottish highlands. 'Not quite the Eye of Orion,' he mused, making his way to the only house for miles – a small neatly constructed stone cottage with a smoking chimney. Despite the time of year on Earth, there was a distinct nip in the clear Inverness air. 'Last time I was here,' recollected the Doctor, 'I met young Jamie – or was it the time before that?'

Inside the cottage Herbert took his position, armed with a copy of the New Testament in one hand and a large crucifix in the other, whisked from the wall in a frenzy. The Doctor knocked, pushing open the door cautiously, to find Herbert threatening him in a totally bizarre manner. The Time Lord bypassed Herbert with a curt gesture of disinterest, finding Vena cowering behind the door.

'Hello, I'm the Doctor. You must be Vena.'

It did not take long for the ex-Maylin's daughter to realise who this was, leaving Herbert continuing his attempts to exorcise an unwanted 'spirit'.

The Doctor sidestepped Herbert's plans to remove his presence by force, and discussed more serious issues with the lady he had come for. Vena was eager for the Doctor's help. She reminded herself how he had saved Karfel once before. A severe famine generations ago nearly wiped out all inhabitants. And it was for this reason that Vena agreed to place the amulet in the Doctor's hands and return to Karfel.

Herbert eventually accepted his visitors' stories. Whether he had summoned them through the glass or not, they were indeed real and had to be the most exciting encounter he had ever experienced in his relatively short and uninteresting lifetime.

'Can I come too, Doctor?' enquired Herbert with a half-smile and polite frown. An answer to his outspoken request quickly dampened his enthusiasm.

'We're not off on some joy-ride, you know young man,' bellowed the Doctor, eager to get back to the TARDIS. 'The situation on Karfel is serious, very serious indeed!'

'Not to mention dangerous,' added Vena grimly.

Herbert retracted, realising that he was on a losing track. He turned to pick up his shoes and jacket then looked at his visitors directly.

'Very well then. It was a pleasure meeting you both. I'm sorry we couldn't have become better acquainted.' The Victorian gentleman then proceeded out of the room into the kitchen, closing the door firmly.

The Doctor tapped Vena on the arm, signalling it was their cue to leave.

'Nice enough lad, but I can't possibly agree to his request.'

The Time Lord spotted a mirror on the oakwood Welsh dresser. He fingered it thoughtfully, then pocketed it. 'Remind me to return it to Herbert when this is all over,' he said.

Vena nodded, and they departed.

The main doors of the Borad's vault slid open to allow his personal android entry. A report was made concerning the captured rebels, and that Peri had also been taken in the arrest. A rather pleased Borad issued further instructions as the android mentally recorded the orders systematically and without emotion.

'Prepare the girl Peri with the M-80 cylinder as we have discussed, and set up a viewer in order that I can observe the experiment closely.'

The android nodded, then paused to consider another matter: 'Borad, what about the Doctor? What shall I do with him when he returns to claim his assistant?'

The mysterious ruler of Karfel mused momentarily. It was obvious that little warmth existed between the two, and the Borad made the command that he had issued on so many occasions.

'Use the Timelash. I have little need of the Time

Lord, since he will have served my purposes. But bring me his time-machine – that will be my prize.'

Vena strolled around the centre console of the TARDIS quite intrigued by the moving parts before her eyes.

'You'll soon have to hang on, my dear,' the Doctor grinned with reassurance. 'Don't worry, it will only be temporary discomfort. Once inside the Timelash corridor it will be plain sailing.'

'Incredible! Absolutely incredible!'

The Doctor gyrated angrily, glaring at the stowaway. 'What in the universe are *you* doing here!'

Herbert, too impressed and elated by his fascinating experience, only offered a rapturous grimace.

'Are we travelling below or above water?'

Whisked aside, the master of the TARDIS soon admonished his 'guest', removing his gleeful expression, after a severe reprimand.

Herbert retreated into a corner with his tail between his legs. 'I promise I won't get in the way, Doctor,' he bleated sheepishly.

Nevertheles, the new time-traveller pulled out his pocket notebook and began furiously compiling notes. Sketches and diagrams were quickly lined in thick pencil as if he were professionally surveying his surroundings.

The TARDIS walls began to tremble. The Doctor shouted to his new companions to brace themselves, and with the accompanying cacophony that alarmed Vena, the time-machine approached the vortex in space.

The TARDIS once more appeared as a blip on the Timelash's tracker screen, and was quickly spotted by Tekker's hawk-eyes.

'You see,' he squealed, entirely pleased with events, 'I told you he'd return.'

Kendron made no reply, and bowed his head over the controls. Soon the faint outline of the TARDIS grew to fuller form in the main chamber as its silhouette materialised fully like a blue monolith.

'He can't do this,' the councillor complained. 'He gave his word, I heard him.'

Brunner, less naïve, scowled at Kendron's weak nature. 'Say much more and you'll be joining the Doctor and his friends in the Timelash. Now get the vortex ready. You heard our Maylin – he wants them all despatched.'

Kendron did as he was bid and the humming of the Timelash gently took its place in the relative silence of the Inner Sanctum. Within minutes it was primed to send more victims into the depths of oblivion.

7

Fight or Perish

The Doctor could hardly wait for the TARDIS doors to open, bowling out like a flash of lightning into the Inner Sanctum with Herbert hot on his heels.

The 'welcoming committee' of Karfelons and guardoliers, spear-headed by the Maylin Tekker, closed ranks. Their faces of gloom contrasted with the last occasion the TARDIS had arrived. Tekker outstretched his long hand and directed his interest to the amulet in the Time Lord's grip.

'I'll take that, Doctor.'

Vena looked daggers at the Karfelon she and her father once trusted. 'Who pulls your strings now, Tekker?' she asked.

The Doctor had other priorities. 'Where's Peri?'

No direct answer was forthcoming.

Herbert, in a world of his own, continued to make endless notes in his pocket book as if he were part of some scientific expedition.

Tekker stood fast and wiggled the ends of his fingers. 'No amulet, no Peri.'

With a sigh of disgust the Doctor sharply ejected the amulet and chain into his adversary's hand, then once more enquired after his companion.

With a single curt wave from the Maylin, the room's lighting dimmed as if all power was being diverted elsewhere. The Timelash doors gradually opened revealing a bright swirling tornado within. The Inner Sanctum doors swung open allowing Mykros, Sezon and Katz to be brought in, each neck-looped to a guardolier. Seven rebels in all faced the fate of uncertainty: the Timelash.

The Doctor turned crimson at such treachery. 'You gave me your word – you microcephalic apostate!'

Tekker merely tendered a sickening grin of satisfaction. He had received precisely what he wanted, completing the Borad's explicit instructions.

'You are all to be subjected to the Timelash,' the Maylin gloated, in a high-pitched cackle. You first, Doctor. It appears the great Time Lord has actually run out of time.'

A single android strode forward and gripped the back of the Doctor's neck without warning, slowly manipulating him towards the dazzling void of the Timelash. Mykros and Vena exchanged fearful glances. It seemed their joyous reunion was to be shortlived. Sezon and Katz boiled over with bitter emotion, powerless to help their ally who was now at the mouth of the time corridor. Within seconds he would be hurled into the vortex to endure an unknown future – if he were to survive the trip at all.

Some distance away, Peri puffed as she was marched to a scientific laboratory displaying a vast array of technical paraphernalia. An elderly Karfelon approached her guardolier and commanded him to release his hold on the prisoner. The Karfelon, whom Peri took for a scientist, produced a small metal canister and body strap which he fitted to her without explanation.

Neck-looped once more, Peri was removed in another direction with the light cylinder firmly in place. Its purpose and content remained a mystery. Peri was undeniably anxious – not only for herself, but for the Doctor too.

The android relentlessly pushed its metal claw into the Doctor's neck, forcing him forward. Oblivion was but a step away. The Time Lord dug deep into his bulging pockets and produced the mirror he had borrowed from Herbert's cabin. Angling a reflection directly into the android's eyes, it shone more than enough light to temporarily blind the creature which automatically released its death grip and allowed the Doctor to break free.

Within seconds the room turned into a war zone as rebels liberated themselves to grapple fiercely with the guardoliers. Tekker diplomatically took his leave at this point, reluctant for further involvement, retreating swiftly out of the chamber. Vena and Herbert smashed the spy camera in the chamber, allowing Sezon to seal the doors and destroy its mechanism, and making the area temporarily impenetrable.

Once more the Doctor found himself on the brink of the Timelash, battling for his life with Brunner and an android. Mykros, who had won his fight, bounded over to assist, and managed to lever first the android and then Brunner into the tunnel that spanned time and space. There was a moment available for a quick handshake and hurried introduction before Mykros raced to aid Katz. The Doctor attended to more technical matters and made his way to the controls of the Timelash itself.

Soon the spacious chamber was littered with guardoliers who had temporarily lost their struggle. Their unconscious bodies were dragged unceremoniously into an antechamber where they were securely incarcerated.

'What is this Timelash, Doctor?' Herbert was soon eyeing the controls with excitement.

'Not now, Herbert, there's too much to do.'

Vena was also interested in what the Doctor was planning, and was surprised to learn of his intention.

'I'm going into the Timelash,' he announced.

The Borad snarled at Tekker's incompetence, issuing him with a stern warning of what would happen if he continued to fail in his duty. The leader's mechanical chair whirled as it carried its gross load around the damp vault. Tekker, pleased to be alive, stepped aside, awaiting further instructions.

'Take the time-web acceleration beam and break into the Inner Sanctum. Dispose of all rebels within, and then bring the Doctor to me. I want him to observe his assistant's fate before I dispose of him personally.'

Tekker smiled, but dared not utter a word. He simply withdrew meekly, bowing his head as he departed, and relishing his duty to challenge the Doctor once more.

Mykros spun some rope around the Doctor's waist securely. 'Can't I go, Doctor?' pleaded Herbert who also stepped forward for a chance to be chosen.

'I'm not going to perform some sort of sporting event!' bellowed the Time Lord, knowing full well the good intentions of Herbert and Mykros. 'I've got to go in on my own. Releasing Kontron crystals is a tricky operation. They require skilful manipulation. Anything less would cause instability and the Timelash could implode!'

Vena wasn't quite sure of the need for these crystals, and so the Doctor reminded her of their strange and powerful properties. They were the only things likely to be of any use against their enemies.

Sezon and Katz hooked up the other end of the line to a pillar, and then they took the strain as the Doctor eased himself into the Timelash opening. Layer upon layer of shimmering light streaked out of the vortex, giving a hypnotic effect to any attracted viewer. Vena was far from happy about the Doctor's plan, but helped him all the same, wishing him luck and success.

Peri felt like crying, though she had experienced a lot worse in her lifetime – especially alongside the Doctor. She thus restrained herself from doing anything that would undermine her ability and affect her self-respect. Gazing around at the gloomy cell that imprisoned her she once again tried to remove the grey canister that was securely fastened about her middle.

Then a thought hit her like a knife stabbing through butter. Could the cylinder be explosive? Did they expect her to organise her own demise? She stopped fingering the device instantly and treated it with extreme caution. Resigned, and unable to do much more, Peri took a seat against a damp wall. She had already shouted for help without any response, and needed to recuperate before trying another line of action. One thing was certain, she could not give up.

The Timelash entrance was the first step into the unknown. The Doctor had never been inside a corridor like this before without the TARDIS to protect him. He squinted below, spying a mass of projecting lithoids. On the end of each he knew would be a Kontron crystal, and two were needed for his purposes. Calling to the others to release more slack on the line, the Doctor began to stretch for the crystal nearest to him.

He could sense the powerful attraction force taking effect as he pushed his way on to one stem. Gingerly, he manoeuvred himself towards the fist-shaped sparkling nugget. There were now only inches to go, but the line prevented him from going any further.

'Let me have more slack!' he shouted, and again he was able to move forward. The Doctor's fingers brushed its target, eventually coming to rest around the crystal itself. He gently manipulated its position, looking back to see his precarious situation. Concentric rings of the vortex swirled endlessly into the depths of the bottomless pit. Finally a multi-crystalline-like structure was firmly in the Time Lord's grasp. 'One down,' he sighed. 'One to go.'

Tekker ordered an android detachment to set up the time-acceleration web outside the Inner Sanctum. The beam was set to disintegrate the doors, and a squad of crack guardoliers stood ready as a mini-attack force. Tekker was becoming edgy. He began to recall the Borad's threat of what would happen to him if he failed. Kendron, who had also fled from the chamber, stood by his side. Tekker mused for a moment. Perhaps he would survive, successful or not.

The vortex attraction forces were rapidly taking effect on the foreign body that fought the flow of the corridor's power and was now about to seize a second crystal. Unfortunately for the Doctor, the second Kontron crystal was proving too elusive and difficult to uncouple from the pentagonal lithoid stretching out to oblivion.

'Can't I come down and help?' cried Herbert from the opening of the Timelash above.

'You stay where you are! I've nearly got the second one.'

An alarming tornado motion then swirled all the projectiles. The Doctor clung on as best he could, finally chancing his arm and grabbing the other prism-like structure. Whipping it into his large coat pocket, the only thing left on his mind was escape, and quickly. An unnatural source of turbulent energy impacted the area taking the weight off the Time Lord's body and suspending him in mid-air. It was merely Mykros's knot around his middle that prevented him from being cast through the eye of the corridor with a one-way ticket.

Sezon and Katz and the others sweated as Herbert watched the events below. He knew something had to be done – and fast. As the Doctor tried his best to regain control on the lashing, Herbert swiftly moved into the corridor and grabbed the line tightly. Then, foolhardy in action, he began making his way down to the Doctor, who shouted at his rescuer's impetuous act of bravery.

'Get back, Herbert! You'll be swept away!'

Mykros then also climbed inside, mainly to keep a hold on Herbert, and a body chain was established. After several close encounters with failure, Herbert eventually grabbed the Doctor's sweating hands and began pulling him up to safety. The group above tugged madly to pull the entire chain out of the Timelash, and after a few anxious moments from Vena's standpoint, Mykros, Herbert and eventually the Doctor, emerged, quite shaken by their experience, but thankfully all in one piece.

A joyous reunion was cut short by an impatient Time Lord. The Doctor reminded them of the many tasks they had yet to accomplish. This was underlined when Katz spotted an invasion force on the planet's tracker screens. Mykros eyed the armada with deep concern.

'Doctor?'

The Time Lord had little to say and continued to work against the clock. He had to convert his spoils of the Timelash into effective instruments of defence if they were to stand any hope of survival.

Peri had nodded off in her cell, and was rudely awoken by the cold touch of the noose device once more introduced about her slender neck. She yelled abuse at the unfeeling guardolier who hauled her upwards like a sack of potatoes. Without explanation the soldier released her from the bars and frogmarched her out.

It wasn't long before Peri's blood chilled with fear. She could detect that smell again. The one she associated with the cave creature. To her horror, the guardolier was leading her out of the Citadel to confront the monster for a second time.

The Doctor fumbled with a collection of pieces from the Timelash. He particularly worked with the Kontron crystals, making one into a hand-held weapon and the second into a device he placed about his neck with a chain. Putting down his screwdriver, he shone his pocket penlight into the crystals and waited. Herbert, entirely fascinated, watched the events with undivided attention, making notes in his pocketbook. After ten seconds the crystalline neckpiece returned the light almost as if it signalled a response.

'It flashes back to you, Doctor,' declared Herbert triumphantly.

'That's what it's supposed to do,' said the Doctor. 'Haven't put one of these together since time school on Gallifrey.'

Katz and Sezon drew closer to see the ultimate experiment. Adjusting the base of the crystal chain, the Doctor sat perfectly still. Then Mykros and Herbert jumped a mile when they were nudged by some unseen force. Katz moved to touch the Doctor in his trance-like state, only to see her hand pass right through him. Then his image stood up and thrust his hand towards Mykros and Herbert. Returning to his seat he turned off the Kontron device. The Doctor was well pleased.

'Come on, Doctor,' said Vena, quite taken with what she'd witnessed. 'What was that about?'

'A ten second time loop,' he declared triumphantly. 'I can send my image ten seconds back in time, leaving my real self totally undetected.'

'Fantastical!' raved Herbert, scribbling furiously. 'It's science –' He paused. 'Yet fiction.'

'Highly factual,' huffed the Doctor who moved on to the hand-weapon he had constructed.

'But how will all this help us, Doctor?' complained Sezon, whose rather brash down-to-earth manner began to raise its ugly head again.

'The Kontron gun we'll use against the first android that comes in here. Perhaps the effect will put off others from moving in. And we've got enough blasters to put a fair fight.'

Katz then had a thought: 'That Kontron gun, Doctor, what will it do to its target?'

'Ignite it by pure energy and send it back in time by about one hour, though I can't vouch for the location yet.'

Katz's spine tingled. She turned to Sezon, who smiled with the same notion. 'The burning android when we rescued Peri from the Morlox,' he beamed.

The Doctor raised one eyebrow. 'Nice to know that it will actually work.'

A burst of time-energy began to eat a hole in the giant doors of the Inner Sanctum Chamber. The rebels darted for cover pointing their weapons towards the disintegrating portals. The Doctor rapidly put his Kontron gun together and set it up as the first wave of guardoliers entered to take a burst of blaster fire. Several were hit in the crossfire, including one of Sezon's team. A heated struggled ensued, the Doctor biding his time despite the pleas of Herbert to fire on the advancing Citadel troops.

Below the fury, deep in the recesses of the Borad's vault, the ruler of Karfel too had spotted the group of Bandril battle cruisers approaching the planet, preparing to destroy the Karfelon inhabitants.

'Excellent,' he wheezed. 'Soon the only living things on this planet will be the Morloxes and myself.'

8

Battle Stations

'*Fire!*' bellowed Herbert in a state of frenzy as he saw an
android enter the beseiged chamber. Calmly the Doctor
primed the Kontron gun and pointed it directly at the
robotic shape. A bolt of light shot out of the Kontron
gun finding its strike position deep within the fabricated
chest of the Borad's slave. Instantaneously the artificial
shell of the android burned vigorously, causing the
entire unit to disintegrate. Within seconds, it had
dematerialised.

Peri screamed her lungs out as she was roughly
manacled once more, this time to a post in front of a
Morlox cave. The penetrating roar of the creature could
be heard within, and quite soon the Doctor's assistant
would again be face to face with salivating jaws and the
fiersome flared nostrils of a carnivore.

The fighting continued, and Sezon was hit by a ricochet
shot, though not too seriously. A further blast hit a spot
just above the Doctor's head, sending plaster in every

direction. Underneath a mural could be seen a painting of the Doctor in a previous incarnation – a white-haired figure sporting a frilly shirt and a fine velvet jacket.

Herbert looked puzzled, but the Doctor had no time to go into the laws of regeneration.

'I wonder,' posed the Time Lord, scratching at another piece of the crumbling wall still under crossfire.

'What?' yapped Herbert, with his head crouched low.

'Not now, I've got to get to the Borad.'

'But what about the invasion force?'

'Borad first, them a close second.'

With that, the Doctor called to Katz and Mykros for cover, and took his chance, darting out of the chamber. As usual, Herbert wasn't far behind, and the pair headed for the vault below the Citadel.

The Borad was busy taking stock of things. Before him stood Tekker and Kendron, summoned because of their failure to contain the rebels. The loss of a prize android was also a matter not be taken lightly.

'I am pleased to say I know how the rebels managed to put up a fight, Borad.'

'Indeed?' he retorted crossly.

'Kendron,' Tekker gesticulated to the councillor at his side. 'He betrayed us by helping the rebels and the Doctor. I'm sorry it has taken so long to flush him out, but he has been unbelievably cunning.'

Kendron stammered in his own defence, but could not utter enough to save his life. A merciless beam of time-accelerated energy tore into the Karfelon's body, invigorating his inner cells to grow old rapidly.

Kendron aged to senility and beyond, to a skeletal shape and further on, finally falling to the floor in a pile of smouldering dust.

Tekker exhaled with relief. He has escaped the wrath of his leader, and lived to fawn again.

The Borad turned his attention to a large screen where Peri faced a chained Morlox. He fingered the 'release' control on the arm of his chair, then restrained his temptation to use it.

'The Doctor should be here soon, there's time enough.' Tekker was far from clear about the girl's fate and the significance of his master's words, but he didn't question. Instead he took his position in the half-light to welcome the Time Lord on arrival.

The Doctor was far from pleased. 'Herbert, in your next life you'd make a wonderful golden retriever.'

'Sorry, Doctor, just thought I could help.'

'I'm sure you think this is one big adventure to be savoured and enjoyed.'

Herbert was tempted to answer 'yes' but thought better of it.

'Well, it's not. The highlight of your visit to Karfel could be a burial in space – with you playing the central part.'

Herbert took the hint, and began to walk back to the Inner Sanctum, but he was stopped.

'Come on, I'm sure I can find something to keep you occupied. I don't want you picked up by guardoliers – it's bad enough losing Peri.' Herbert wanted to smile broadly, but contented himself with a camouflaged grin.

He paced on behind his hero, only too pleased to be part of events.

Finally the pair found themselves outside a large double door without a guard.

'Funny,' remarked the Doctor. 'Why no resistance? It's as if I'm being given an open invitation.'

As Herbert turned to make notes, the Borad's vault opened to allow the visitor to enter, and then shut fast.

Not wanting to be totally left out, Herbert climbed a ladder at the corner of the corridor. To his delight it led to a tiny gantry where he could look down and actually see the Doctor inside the vault. But what was in the high-backed chair on the other side of the darkened room?

The Time Lord knew instinctively that his life was now very definitely at risk. He became curious all the same and spotted a grey cylinder left on a table near the doors. Sniffing the top nozzle, he immediately identified the contents of the canister.

Tekker crept out to confront his adversary, but the Doctor showed little interest in him. 'Still lurking in other people's shadows, Tekker? How very typical.'

Tekker pointed his hand-blaster at the Borad's visitor in order to emphasise his advantage, and the Doctor's disadvantage. 'Welcome, Doctor.'

A strong sickly aroma clung to the vault like honey, a point immediately picked up by the Time Lord. Tekker noticed the Doctor's senses working on the smell, and gave him the answer he was trying to recall: 'Morlox.'

'Of course – the creatures of the tunnels. I remember them from my last visit. So your leader is a Morlox?'

Tekker showed scorn of the Doctor's dry wit.

'Where is he then? The one who calls himself the Borad?' said the Time Lord.

A deep satanic voice echoed from one corner of the dark chamber as the mechanical chair rolled into view. The profile of the occupant was far from handsome, but there was the rugged features of a somewhat obese Karfelon – nothing like the old man often seen on the Citadel screens. Slowly the chair moved even further forward, beginning to turn, and as it did so the face of the Karfelon altered dramatically. For the first time Tekker and the Doctor were about to glimpse the real creature in total control of the giant planet.

Peri realised that a chain held the horrific monster back, but even so, she could not take much more of the terror that seared through every bone of her body. The thought of the Morlox breaking free was too awful to contemplate. Her thoughts rested on another rescue from Sezon perhaps, or the Doctor, if he was still alive.

Back in the Inner Sanctum Mykros tried to make contact with the flagship of the Bandril invasion force, but without any success. The planet's fate was sealed. Doom was but a short while away.

There in the shadows of the vault, the Borad's full face was revealed to Tekker and the Doctor, the latter showing interest while Tekker was visibly shocked.

The Borad, and ruler of Karfel, was a merged mutant,

half-Karfelon, half-Morlox. One side bore the features of a once-handsome humanoid, but now he shared such looks with those of a Morlox – protruding eyes, nose and jaw, with a half set of carnivorous teeth. Similarly, the mutant had mixed combinations of arms and flippers, fingers and claws. In Tekker's mind he was looking at a living nightmare, but, to the Doctor, there was something more sinister.

Herbert, who continued to observe the proceedings from far above, crossed himself in a nervous religious act. For him, he was witnessing the devil – Satan himself.

'And you said your leader wasn't a Morlox.'

For once Tekker didn't have a response. He continued to study the Borad.

'So what went wrong, Borad? I can't believe you look like this by choice,' said the Doctor.

The Borad moved into an area of light, highlighting his gruesome features. 'An agreeable mistake,' he said.

The Doctor pointed to the cylindrical container: 'Mustakozene 80. Don't tell me you've been playing around with that?' The Doctor turned to Tekker, who looked queasy. 'M80 – the most unstable element in this galaxy.'

'Right,' agreed the Borad, eager to defend his appearance. 'Yet it was such a happy transformation. I have the strength of many, and intelligence that outstrips the most intelligent Karfelon.'

'But hardly the looks to match.'

'Looks, Doctor? What are looks when I control all, and have longevity that will even outlive you and your countless regenerations?'

The Time Lord was curious about the Borad's familiarity. 'Do I know you?'

The mutant bid him to come closer. 'Now look carefully. Think back to a scientist you befriended but eventually reported to the Inner Sanctum for unethical experimentation on Morlox creatures.'

Suddenly it was clear to the Doctor who this Karfelon was: Megelen, once known as mad Megelen.

A story unfolded as to how Megelen has been sprayed accidentally by M80 while using it experimentally on a Morlox. The creature broke free and partially ingested the scientist, forming a combined mutant, half-Karfelon and half-Morlox.

'But what good is all this to you?' the Doctor continued to reason, now near the truth. 'You dare not ever show your face on the planet you rule. Instead we see the face of an old man, probably an android. Am I right?'

The Borad remembered the Doctor's direct persuasive ways and retracted slightly.

The Time Lord reflected. He was determined to work out the details rather than have them handed to him on a plate. The invasion had something to do with it, though no civilisation and a barren planet made little sense.

'No Karfelons, quite right. But barren? Not for long,' said the Borad.

Tekker had come to a quick conclusion. He realised he had been working towards the destruction of his own race. Despite his treacherous nature, that was something he could not support. Turning the blaster towards the Borad, he lingered a second too long before releasing his shot. A bright channel of accelerated time left the arm control of the Borad's seat of power. Tekker froze, encapsulated by the force he could do little to stop. He aged rapidly, crumbling where he stood, until all that remained in his ashes were his amulet and blaster.

The Doctor applauded mockingly. 'A time-acceleration beam. I don't know whether to be impessed or disgusted.'

'Enough, Doctor. Before I rid you from my vaults I'll let you see my latest experiment, though fundamentally this one has already been tried and tested. Real evidence of the workability of a process to generate new life on this planet.' The mutant responded to the Doctor's puzzled look.

Activating the view-screen, the Borad showed Peri's impending date with a female Morlox. Around her was a cylinder of M80.

'You can't be serious!' the Time Lord gasped, horrified, obtaining a contorted chuckle in response.

'Soon Peri and I will begin creating our own species. A glorious transformation for a new Karfel.'

The Doctor reached for the Kontron crystal around his neck. It was time to release Peri from the clutches of the evil ruler.

The Borad, sensing a move afoot, reached for the chain release to activate his controlled experiment.

'No!' warned the Doctor, knowing the awful consequences for his innocent assistant.

Turning the base of the Kontron crystal, the Time Lord raced to try and find the release button for Peri. Immediately he was fired upon, though only his ten-second image was hit.

Herbert, terrified, clutched the cross chain around

his neck and prayed devoutly. He knew the Doctor had to survive or it would be the end of Peri, Karfel and all its inhabitants.

Without much success, the Doctor shut off his 'toy', returning to true time.

'So you want to play games, Doctor?' The Borad's tone became intimidating. 'Try using that again!' he warned. He prepared to squeeze his time-web trigger once more.

'Don't you dare,' warned the Doctor. 'You're aiming at a Kontron crystal. It's suicide.'

The Borad was unimpressed, 'Goodbye, Doctor, keep your bluff.'

'You'll kill yourself!' insisted the Time Lord with open sincerity.

A further beam of energy was swiftly despatched from the Borad's chair, hitting its target squarely on the chest, but nothing happened. The streak of power was simply consumed inside the crystal hanging loosely about the Doctor's neck. The Time Lord pouted, shaking his head. The Kontron crystal began to glow brightly, becoming even brighter until it shone a brilliant white. The energy was about to return to its source, and the Borad knew it.

'Doctor!' the pathetic mutant screeched. 'You've tricked me!'

The source of energy like a bolt of lightning flashed out from the crystal and boomeranged back to the Borad, slicing into him at the speed of light. A cacophonous noise ended the mutant's life, leaving a pyramid-shaped pile of dust in the seat of the motor-driven chair. The Doctor passed final judgement. 'You tricked yourself.'

Herbert still had his eyes closed when he heard his name being called. 'Who is it?' he croaked, quaking in his shoes.

'It's me! Who do you think?' growled the Doctor impatiently. 'Get outside to Peri and try and free her. I'll try and find the chain release from in here.'

Herbert cautiously opened his eyes and, refusing to look down, slid out of the walkway, obeying the Doctor's instructions. The Time Lord himself tried various switches, until the third one he pressed was indeed a chain release – but the one that controlled the chain of the Morlox. Glancing sideways at the screen, the Doctor observed the female Morlox break free and lumber towards a screaming Peri.

9

Regrouping

Herbert darted out onto the planet's parched surface. Directed by Peri's shrill cries, he met the full-sized Morlox, not dissimilar in looks to the half-crature he had seen in the vault. Looking around hurriedly he found a large piece of wood once used as a stake and rushed forward, jabbing it into the face of the snarling creature. The animal, reluctant to be put off its meal, bit at the rescuer's weapon viciously in an attempt to eradicate it from the duel. Herbert gripped the stake for all he was worth.

The Doctor made his way down the main lower corridor also following his ears, but was stopped in his tracks by the Borad's personal android programmed to kill. Its bright green eyes ignited like hot coals as the creature raised both arms to attack. Looking behind, there was little to gain by a tactful retreat, especially in the maze of endless corridors. Fumbling in his pockets, the Doctor pulled out a pocket penknife and removed the Kontron necklace. By a quick two second adjustment the crystals began to heat and smoulder. Thrusting them directly towards the advancing android, the Kontron crystals stuck fast to the chest of the advancing creature and began to eat a hole in its tunic and chest. With a new problem to occupy its program, the Doctor slipped by the smoking android as it fell hard to the ground, wriggling for its existence.

Continuing his path outside, he bolted to help Herbert who was quickly losing ground, as well as his wooden weapon.

The Bandril ships had increased in number on the central scanner. Vena had counted them as twenty-two – a complete battle complement.

'It's no use,' insisted Mykros, 'they just won't answer my signals. I've tried every channel and frequency. I wish the Doctor would come back and help us.'

'I'm sure he would if he could,' replied Katz, who watched the doors in case of a surprise return of guardoliers.

'Where is everyone?' Vena asked, strolling over to Katz's vantage point.

'Perhaps the Doctor has relieved the Borad of his command. No guardoliers must mean something's up,' suggested Katz.

Vena wasn't so optimistic. She felt it could mean a final regrouping before they were all slaughtered where they stood.

Peri was practically free now, but still pinned down. Removing his jacket, Herbert wrapped it around the stake. The Doctor supplied a light and the wooden wrap was used as a flaming torch to be thrust into the jaws of the agitated Morlox. This left time for Herbert to remove the cylinder very carefully from around Peri, and then stand it upright on the ground.

'Run!' was the order to Peri who needed little encouragement.

'What about you two?' asked the young American.

'We'll be along,' shouted Herbert, who noticed the flames were nearly out. 'Now what, Doctor?'

The Doctor lifted the M80 cylinder and unscrewed the top very slowly. Getting Herbert to drop the wooden stake, he sprayed the length of it with the dangerous element, leaving one end free from the unstable chemical. Containing the cylinder once more, he lay it to one side, lifting the stake like a javelin; and with one almighty lunge projected the wooden stick straight into the open mouth of the snapping Morlox.

What happened next was quite remarkable. The Morlox amalgamated with the wood, the latter growing and expanding in every direction. Large stakes protruded from every part of the animal's body like a vast network of new bones. The effect meant instant death for the Morlox and a reminder to the Doctor of mustakozene's power and instability.

Herbert's colour lightened, as he tried not to look at the contorted mess left behind at the cave's entrance.

'Sorry, old boy, but I had to do it. It was her or us. She would have stopped playing with us and made me the main course, and you the dessert,' said the Doctor. Herbert nodded and they rejoined Peri inside the lower corridor.

'Am I pleased to have you back, Doctor,' Peri said, delighted.

'The feeling's quite mutual. Now come on, back to the Inner Sanctum. We've a war to stop.'

Mykros and the others welcomed the Doctor back, though any smiles were short-lived as all that filled the minds of those in the Inner Sanctum chamber were the flashing symbols representing battleship positions. It would only be a matter of time now before missiles were launched and Karfel's inhabitants destroyed. All because of a ruthless dictator's mental state of balance. A ruler who no longer existed.

A chorus of invasion alarms echoed repeatedly around the chamber as an array of warning lights signalled danger for the Citadel.

'I forgot about those,' noticed Vena, 'though they're a bit late.'

Mykros wasn't so sure. 'Aren't they warning of an attack on the key areas of the Citadel?'

Vena nodded. But from *within* Karfel?' There was an elongated pause. 'You're right. An attack has been launched on our doorstep. It can't be Bandrils surely?'

The Doctor edged over to see what the commotion was about. 'Looks like a large detachment of soldiers is about to attack this area. Could there have been an advance party?'

'Impossible,' concluded Mykros, who was now checking for more details, 'Look!'

There on the internal tracking system about fifty troopers were moving into the Inner Sanctum area.

'Guardoliers?' queried Herbert.

'These are androids.'

'All fifty of them?' declared the Doctor with surprise. 'I thought the Borad only had a handful.'

'So did we all.' Mykros looked around the chamber. They had little to fight with now. It seemed the Borad had organised a large battle reserve to polish off all the Karfelons in the Citadel if ever he was outwitted by the rebels.

'His legacy to us all,' thought Vena soberly.

'How long have we got?'

'Ten minutes if that. They're marching from the western perimeter. He must have had them in silos deep underground.'

It was certain that these androids would be killers shaping the fate of all those present. The choice was clear: assassination by androids or bombing by invaders. The Doctor knew the TARDIS could save them, but what of all the other inhabitants of the planet? There had to be a way out.

10

Legacy of the Borad

Citadel dwellers scattered in droves as the ominous marching sound of military might surfaced from the western perimeter. Well-armed androids in silver suits crashed their way on a direct route to the Inner Sanctum chamber. There was no resistance, and the sight of the tightly knit unit of killers was ample reason for any Karfelon to retreat or escape from their line of approach.

The Doctor had already attempted to find a solution by returning to the Borad's vault. He was only able to discover that the fifty-strong detachment were programmed to destroy all living creatures in their path in or out of the Citadel. Even if it took them a thousand cycles of the planet's galactic orbit, the troops would continue to hunt, seek out and destroy.

Sezon and Katz tried to organise some weapons, the former still recovering from a blast injury to his right shoulder. They were trained to fight to the last, and that is precisely what they intended to do. Vena still tried to contact the Bandril, but with little success.

Mykros ran with the Doctor to try and find more weapons, but the Time Lord knew that not to be the answer.

'How about some more of your Kontron crystals, Doctor?'

'Impossible.' The Doctor was quite definite. 'After removing two of them the corridor will be totally unstable. I'd never get out of there alive a second time. No, there's got to be another way.'

'But what? How can we stop these powerful creatures, Doctor? They have the might of ten of us.'

Both of them thought deeply of the predicament and it took a few pensive moments for the Doctor to finally sparkle with an idea that had some small hope.

'Mykros – the power vaults. Where are they?'

'I can take you there, Doctor, if it's not too late.'

'Explain.'

'Well, they're in the central sector. The androids will be near to that area now.' It sounded very risky.

'If we get into the vaults – can they break in?'

'No way, Doctor. The vault doors are totally impregnable. The Borad saw to that.'

It seemed the only course of action, but Mykros knew that the only way in meant the use of the amulets, a fact that he was quick to point out to his ally.

'Is that all we need?' muttered the Doctor in a glib tone. 'You forget I have spent at least twenty minutes and two visits in the Borad's vault. I have both the amulets with me.'

The Time Lord nodded Mykros forward and the pair rushed through the range of corridors at speed. Mykros knew the Citadel very well and used a few short cuts to reach the power vaults quickly.

The power area was a relatively tiny complex and

once the amulets had been inserted into their respective slots at the doors, the sturdy metal portals whisked open to allow them access. As soon as the two intruders had crossed the threshold, once again the thick metallic doors sealed them inside.

Mykros tried to remember the sequence of events when he was last in the chamber with Maylin Renis. He allowed himself a split second to reflect on that time, sad that his would-be father-in-law had been assassinated by the force that thrived on the energy that flowed from the bowels of that very room.

'Come on, Mykros,' rattled the Doctor impatiently, 'we haven't got all day.'

The young Karfelon blinked and set his mind to the task of opening the power panels by simultaneous use of the amulets. As with the Timelash, he was overawed by the sight that presented itself to him. Shimmering lights in multi-colours and effects – the tip of gargantuan reserves of power all held compactly below the level of this control room.

'My, my,' commented the Doctor, who was also impressed. 'Our departed leader had been busy.'

'But also very greedy, Doctor. Did you know he even made Remis switch all power from the hospitals?'

The Time Lord nodded. 'He became hungry. Power was a drug he could not relinquish. But we haven't come here to spout the evil-minded dicatator's epitaph.'

Mykros shook his head in agreement, but was now very much out of his depth as the Doctor began removing one of the panels.

'Are you sure you know what you are doing?' asked Mykros.

The Doctor failed to answer the question and continued his task, grunting as he broke into a sweat which was mainly due to the intense heat generated by the open panels. 'If I can short-circuit these power lines...' The Time Lord stopped to catch his breath, realising the extreme danger involved in his risky endeavours. Mykros could sense the gamble but with the entire planet's population on the brink of total annihilation, the prevailing dangers seemed of little consequence.

'Is there anything I can do, Doctor?'

'Yes, tell me how far the android battalion is from their target.' Frantic activity at the open panel continued as Mykros worked out some figures with his chronographer. His conclusion was approximately three minutes. The android army would probably be visible now in the Citadel's central corridor.

Peri armed herself with a blaster, tucking herself tightly into a corner of the Inner Sanctum near the Timelash. She reasoned that a flight in the vortex with the prospect of twelfth-century Earth as the final resting place for the remaining years of her life, was a preferable option to death by strangulation.

Katz joined her, also armed to the teeth. 'I pray our weapons will work,' she said.

Peri forced a smile. 'We'll be all right.'

Katz cocked her weapon in readiness. 'Mind you, Peri, I must be honest and tell you we only have enough ammunition to stop the first dozen or so. Then –'

Peri held her hand in front of Katz's mouth, who took

the hint and changed the subject.

'Listen!' Sezon commanded silence in the chamber as all the rebels stopped their activity. The beat of marching filtered through the air, growing progressively louder and more threatening. No comments were necessary as the small unit of freedom fighters positioned themselves for the final conflict. Sezon slid beside Katz, recognising her as an equal. They shared the same thought of respect and friendship, joining hands in a gesture of unified camaraderie, while the rhythmic drone of impending doom pulsated in the ears of the waiting fighters.

Mykros was sorely tempted to run back to Vena, sensing that his beloved's end was but a few moments away. Yet the Doctor was now using him as a second pair of hands, and he acknowledged the fact. He would stay at his station for as long as the Time Lord and fate would allow, even though his mind was with Vena.

The temperature in the confines of the power vault had escalated to an almost unbearable level. The Doctor's face was crimson, and his colourful jacket wet through with perspiration. Mykros observed the famous Time Lord under stress, and could see through this struggle that the Doctor was undoubtedly brave and a caring individual, prepared to risk his own existence to save the lives of others. It was probably this basic fact alone that kept Mykros where he was, resolutely supporting and nurturing the last ditch attempt to stop the Borad's legacy of destruction.

Like the clatter of pounding sledgehammers, a vast force of battle androids, moving forward five abreast and brandishing spiked clubs, appeared at the end of the corridor that led to the Inner Sanctum. Programmed to kill all life on Karfel beginning at the Citadel's nerve centre, the powerfully constructed army marched on and were now only a few feet away from the disintegrated portals of the council chamber.

Sezon's team, together with Peri, Herbert and Vena, watched, entirely mesmerised by the numbing sight of vicious mechanical monsters devoid of control.

The rebels' leader bellowed a 'present arms' instruction above the intimidating furore. Herbert, positively terrified, began firing his hand-weapon prematurely, missing his target and wasting valuable ammunition. Yet there was no time to admonish him as, seconds later, Sezon screamed the order everyone was waiting for: '*Fire!*'

A volley of shots echoed through the area directed at the first line of advancing warriors. Four of the five androids took blaster power as direct hits on their streamlined chest pieces, but with little effect. The Borad had created an invincible group of crack killers whose ranks were already two deep into the Inner Sanctum.

The Doctor struggled to unloop the final circuit he was manipulating within his wet grasp. 'Nearly there, Mykros,' he gasped, knowing full well that he had run out of time. Mykros looked at his chronographer. A new digit display marked the end of hope for the Inner

Sanctum. Distraught and upset he released his hold on the opened unit in his grasp, jogging the Time Lord's elbow, sending his screwdriver down into one of the power control boxes.

'Mykros!' barked the Doctor, horrified. 'What have you done?'

The first line of androids stopped in front of Sezon and some of his group, while the second line of five allocated themselves on a one-to-one basis with Vena, Herbert and Katz. The others marched on through the chamber looking for more life forms, allowing the execution party to carry out their first programmed task.

Sezon tried close fire and then ramming one of the androids, only to be thrown on the floor himself. All the metallic creatures raised their spiked death clubs high into the air as Peri closed her eyes. She had forgotten all about the Timelash, and it was too late now anyway. Like seals to be culled, the maces were angled over the heads of the cowering group. The leading android signalled completion of the slaughter, and the solid metal clubs fell with full force unmercifully downwards, but only halfway to their targets. The hum of the androids' power packs stopped, as did marching in other areas. All was quiet.

Katz opened her eyes to see a fat wedge of steel a head's length away from her own. She jumped to her feet around the bristling weapon joined by the others. The fierce execution squad had become frozen statues, quite lifeless and entirely useless. Peri smiled.

'Well done, Doctor.'

11

The Bandrils' Bomb

Mykros stared at the black lifeless interior of the power box nearest the Doctor.

'You do realise I was very attached to that screwdriver, don't you?'

'Sorry Doctor, but it seems that it did the trick.'

'Trick?' queried the Time Lord, moving back from the power panels. '*Trick?*' he snapped, rubbing the sweat from his forehead. '*Trick!*' he shouted, humbling poor Mykros, who recoiled. 'I know I'm looked upon as a magician by some, but it's pure science I deal in, I'll have you know, not cheap tricks.'

Mykros apologised, tongue in cheek, and closed the power panels. 'How did you know that one controlled the androids, Doctor?'

'I guessed.'

They moved out of the vault back into the corridor. Mykros sealed the doors once more.

'And I assume that none of those metal giants will harm or endanger anyone any more?'

The Doctor paused to get his bearings. He surveyed the area to see several doors leading off the strip of walkway. 'Where do these lead, Mykros?'

'Oh, just technical rooms, Doctor, and storage for the Borad's personal androids.'

The Time Lord's curiosity bit and he ventured to the first door. Mykros, on the other hand, was eager to get back to see if Vena was all right, and he was also concerned about the Bandrils.

Opening the door, the two of them walked into the damp area, and along to another inner chamber. This door was cold – very cold.

'Some sort of refrigeration complex. Your food storage?' quizzed the Doctor, quite intrigued by the possibilities.

Mykros shook his head, fearing that any response would delay them further.

Trying the door, there seemed no way in, until it became obvious that the amulets would have to be used once more. The Doctor goaded Mykros into opening up the cold store – a sharp contrast to the parched environment of the power vault. The Time Lord entered the chilly room to see rows and rows of canisters. Each canister was about six feet high and three feet broad. There was a small square glass front to each which was frozen over.

'This isn't food, Mykros. I only hope it's not what I think it is.'

At this stage Mykros had become quite interested by the Doctor's find and began scratching at the iced glass to see what was inside each sealed container.

'By the Gods!' he yelled, catching the sight of the contents. 'What is it, Doctor?'

Sezon and Vena manned the communication controls, attempting to call the Bandril task force, as Katz monitored the scan-screen which was littered with the flashing positions of each craft in the Bandril invasion fleet.

'Wish the Doctor'd get back,' complained Peri to Herbert, who sat making further notes of events and items around him.

'What are you up to Herbert?' asked Peri, her American accent strongly contrasting with Herbert's precise English articulation.

'I'm a writer, you know. Can never turn down the chance to put my ideas on paper. It's so exciting, wouldn't you agree?'

Peri smiled at his naïvety, but refused to shatter his train of thought.

'Must be very exciting travelling through time and space with the Doctor, Peri,' Herbert continued.

'Most of the time,' she offered guardedly. 'I only hope we survive to travel some more. I'd even consider the Eye of Orion right now.'

'Where?'

'Oh, some other time, Herbert. When those blips on the screen stop and turn back, perhaps.'

The Doctor's suspicions were well-founded. He peered into the tall white metal casket to see the gruesome features of the Borad – or more accurately *a* Borad.

'He's been cloning.'

Mykros looked puzzled.

'Reproducing his cells to recreate himself,' explained

the Doctor.

'I don't understand, Doctor. First you tell me that we've been obeying a disfigured half-Morlox, then you say he has actually recreated himself –' Mykros spun on his heels to count the canisters present '– twenty-four times?'

'The puzzle is taking shape, young Mykros. It explains a great deal.'

'Not to me.'

'Time enough. What we must do is stop wasting it here though, and get back to the others. Come on.'

The Inner Sanctum had been cleared of the eight androids. Without power their shells had become light and harmless.

Peri squealed with delight to see the Doctor back, as Mykros met Vena at the door to embrace her once more.

'Doctor, they just won't answer.'

'Indeed? We'll soon see about that. Open a channel for me.'

'You're wasting your breath, Doctor,' Katz piped up. 'They're bent on using a bendalypse warhead, and after what the Borad has subjected them to, I don't blame them.'

The Time Lord regally stalked to the communication podium near the Timelash controls. With both hands firmly clasping his wide lapels, he addressed the screen.

'This is the Doctor calling the Bandril fleet. I say again, this is the Doctor of Gallifrey calling the Bandril fleet. Connect me with the ambassador.' The Time Lord paused, then bellowed, *'Immediately!'*

There was still no response, and the Doctor became impatient. 'I demand to speak with the Bandril ambassador, or you'll have more than a petty war on your hands. You are linked with the President of the High Council of Gallifrey. Kill me and your planet will have them to answer to!'

The intimidating statement worked. A diplomatic channel opened and the Bandril ambassador took the air. 'How do we know you are who you say you are?'

'Trust. The Borad no longer rules this planet. He's dead and his evil regime is over. I give you my word, as a Time Lord.'

The Bandril diplomat conferred before delivering his response. After the suffering and anguish endured by their planet, they were not about to handle matters lightly.

'Before we negotiate any further, prove to us the Borad is dead. Where is his body?'

The Doctor cursed his luck, and the staunch suspicion of the Bandrils. How was he going to explain that the face they knew to be the Borad was that of an android, and that the real dictator was no more than a pile of dust?

'It can't be done, Ambassador. Send down a party and we'll explain. But do not use your missile on this innocent planet.'

The response to the Doctor's plea was sharp and firmly announced. The ambassador stressed his planet's position and totally rejected the Time Lord's proposal. And, just as Tekker had once treated him, he closed the channel, abruptly leaving a black screen in front of the gathered viewers.

Katz howled across the room, attracting the attention of everyone. 'They've gone and done it! The warhead's been ejected from their spearhead group. We're finished.'

Sezon dashed to the screen to see a red streak of cruising light on target for Karfel, travelling at attack speed.

The Doctor snapped his heels together, refusing to answer Peri's barrage of questions. Then, deciding what he had to do, he raced out of the chamber in a flurry.

It didn't take long for the Doctor to locate the TARDIS and activate the central console. Peri was hot on his heels and burst in, much to the Time Lord's annoyance.

'What are you doing, Doctor?'

'Saving my rotten neck,' he replied, giving a look that his assistant intantly identified as sarcasm. 'Now would you please get out of here, young lady? You're distracting me!'

Peri was indignant and rolled her sleeves up to do verbal battle.

'It's no good, Peri, I need to work alone, and there's only minutes to spare. Now *please,* leave me to get on.'

'But I can help you Doctor. I won't get in your way.' The Doctor tripped across her feet in his effort to make some quick adjustments. He looked daggers at the source of his annoyance.

'Get out!' he bellowed, half-losing his voice in the process.

'Can't you tell me what you are up to first?'

The Doctor ignored the distraction and continued his work regardless, but Peri persisted in forcing him to stop once more and face her interrogation.

'Look, Peri, can't you – just this once – accept that I am trying to save us all from a fate no less that total destruction, and can't you see that you are preventing me from succeeding?' Peri backed off a little, although she still refused to budge from the console room. Suddenly with a concentrated effort, the Doctor bodily lifted his young assistant, swiftly carrying her to the door. Her struggles to be put down prevented the Doctor from completing the full task of total eviction. Peri fumed, unaccustomed to the Doctor behaving in this manner. Yet it was precisely because of this that Peri decided that enough was enough. She looked to him for some glimmer of explanation but he looked away with his nose in the air.

Entirely aggravated by his mood, his fiery young assistant stormed out, leaving a contented Time Lord to work, swiftly setting co-ordinates.

'You will be all right, won't you, Doctor?'

The Time Lord glared at Peri's reappearance and bawled vociferously, *'Get out!'*

Ensuring the doors to the TARDIS were now locked, the Doctor activated the necessary controls to de-materialise the time-craft into a orbit pattern around Karfel. Unknown to the Doctor, Herbert had also sneaked on board and positioned himself comfortably underneath the console. His pencil shook furiously between his fingers as he continued to make notes in his rapidly filling jotter. It was the Doctor's foot making contact with Herbert's arm that brought matters to a head between them.

Herbert crawled out apologetically, but there was no

time at that moment for any communication from the Doctor. Herbert's questions fell on deaf ears until all the programming was over and the Time Lord could step back.

'Tell me now, Doctor, what have you been doing?'

The Doctor activated the TARDIS scanner. 'See that?'

Herbert nodded.

'That's a bendalypse warhead.'

'Looks like it's about to hit us.'

The Doctor was very dry with his answer. 'It is.'

'You mean?'

'Yes. The TARDIS will take the full impact, Karfel will be saved, and the Bandrils will realise I was telling the truth.'

Herbert, very impressed, scratched the facts on paper but suddenly looked up with realisation. 'And us, Doctor?'

'Ah, well –'

Herbert didn't want to hear any more. He walked briskly to the Time Lord and give him a firm handshake. 'It was nice knowing you, Doctor. Really. If I have to sacrifice my life to save a planet's population from extinction, then I am pleased to die by your side.'

The Doctor removed his fob watch, reading from the sweeping seconds-hand, then snapped it shut.

'Three seconds,' he announced grimly.

An almighty explosion turned the stratosphere in Karfel's heavens a bright shade of pink. All present in the Inner Sanctum witnessed the event with surprise.

Quite soon Katz saw the Bandril fleet stop their approach and she realised along with the others that the attack had been aborted. Mykros and Vena danced around the room as Sezon breathed an exaggerated sigh of relief. The frenzy spread as Peri too shook hands with one and all.

The repeated call signal from the diplomatic channel was eventually answered by a buoyant Mykros.

'This is the Bandril ambassador.'

'Hallo, Ambassador. Thank you for believing us and terminating your missile.

There was a pause.

'We didn't.' A rapid silence replaced the joyous sounds that had filled the chamber. 'It was the Doctor's unselfish act that caused the missile to be deflected from its target, but I must tell you that it was a direct hit. Our trackers confirm this.'

Peri was stunned, tears welling up in her eyes and streaming down her cheeks.

'May I suggest we send a diplomatic party down? There is much to discuss,' continued the ambassador.

Mykros gave his instant agreement to the request, stabbing at the communication button. Katz and Vena rallied support and their commiserations to Peri, but she rejected all attempts at consolation, walking off into a corner to sit and pull herself together.

Sezon ordered a handful of his group to tidy themselves up to meet the Bandril diplomats. A reception with their neighbours was last entered into fourteen years ago, and history was about to be made.

Vena and Mykros were lost. So long had they accepted instructions that the prospect of sudden freedom and leadership took them by surprise. Mykros was the obvious choice for a temporary Maylin before democratic elections could be held once more, while Katz contented herself with the prospect of returning to her administrative job. She had an inkling that the department she would return to would somehow be a little more challenging. Perhaps Karfel's defence forces?

A stertorous cry, promptly muffled, originated from Peri's corner. The others looked back to see Peri's ugly predicament and Vena held a hand over her mouth in horror. Mykros instantly recognised the grotesque shape holding Peri at bay. It was the Borad.

'Katz, quick, fetch me a blaster,' he cried.

'I wouldn't bother,' grated the yawping voice of the half-Karfelon mutant. 'Not if you want Peri to stay alive.'

Peri squealed as the monstrosity tightened his iron grip across her mouth, forcing Mykros to warn the others not to move or interfere. 'I thought you were dead, Borad.'

'So did I.' Everyone turned round. It was the Doctor. He bounced into the chamber full of life, to the enormous joy of everyone except Peri who was a little tied up with another matter. Mykros, delighted to see the Time Lord, stepped aside to let the Doctor through.

12

Double Trouble

Peri's face reddened as she gasped for air. The Doctor paced gingerly forward until he did not dare go any further.

'You have made a remarkable recovery, Borad,' said the Doctor, evaluating the mutant threatening his assistant's life.

'The trouble with clones, Doctor, is that they never seem to enjoy the same mental attributes as their original counterparts,' rasped the Borad.

The Time Lord smirked. 'Your clone fell for the double bluff and my Kontron crystal remarkably easily, I must admit.' The Doctor looked into the Borad's evil eyes. 'Though it says little for your courage, sending a clone in your place!'

Peri squealed in reaction to the Borad's displeasure at the inferred statement being made.

'Simply a ruse, Doctor, nothing more. Besides I am standing before you now.'

'With the situation as it stands, I do believe you are, you miserable mutation.' The Borad grunted at the Doctor's change of attitude, and also became aggressive.

'In two minutes the girl dies.'

'Impossible, Borad. I can't accept that.'

'In two minutes the girl dies,' he repeated.

The Doctor paced the floor. 'After you tried to turn her into your female counterpart? Do you want her for your bride, or simply dead?'

'I want you to destroy the diplomatic ship when it lands, or I will be agreeing to your latter question, Doctor.'

Mykros strode forward to confer with the Doctor. He stressed the consequences of such an act, but the Doctor knew only too well: a reversal of the situation and another bendalypse warhead targeted on the Karfel people.

'It's madness, Doctor,' declared Katz, keeping her eyes on the creature as she edged forward. 'Why have a war? What'll it achieve?'

The Time Lord backed off but resumed his attention to the Borad.

'Let me tell you all, since I suspect your former ruler – and I stress former – is too pompous to enlighten you himself. Firstly, the annihilation of all Karfelons gives this mad monster an empty land to rule. Secondly, this allows him to repopulate it with beings not dissimilar to himself. Thirdly, he then has no reason to hide himself away. Fourthly, his advances in time would give him power to beat the Bandrils and most other civilisations in this part of the galaxy. The thing is, he'll never achieve any of it as long as he has a half-green snout and a tail between his legs.'

Vena announced the departure of the Bandril ship from its mother craft which was orbiting the planet. This was a cue for the Borad to demand action to his request. His plan was to charge the leading pad with explosives and set a trembler for auto-detonation as soon as the craft made contact with the landing jetty.

'We can't do this, Doctor,' cried Mykros. 'As much as I like Peri, we are committing suicide if the diplomats are killed!'

The Bandril scout craft carrying the ambassador and three other diplomats could be seen as a speck in the sky from the landing pad. Sezon and his comrades packed the area with explosives, setting three trembler switches as instructed. Sezon reported back on his communicator that everything had been carried out as instructed.

In a few minutes the craft would be touching down.

The Doctor had to play the hand he was planning, though things were in a delicate state of equilibrium. The Time Lord knew too well that a squeeze of the Borad's ugly claw could produce the effect of asphyxia in seconds.

'So Borad, the charges are set. Now release Peri.'

'I'm no fool, Doctor, despite what you may think, and I must remind you that you are not addressing a clone either.'

The Doctor swiftly picked up on that very remark. 'Glad to hear it. This ensures the next point I make strikes the target it's aimed at.' Picking up a council chair, the Time Lord advanced with it.

'No closer, Doctor. If you try and throw that at me, you may as well say goodbye to Peri right now ...'

Their task at the landing pad accomplished, Sezon and his colleagues had now entered the chamber and witnessed the events with concern. Holding the chair above his head with a bit of a struggle, the Doctor threw the object sideways, against the wall, where some of the plaster had been shot away by the previous battle. Sheets of wall-covering splintered and cascaded into hundreds of pieces, revealing a giant mirror that had been bricked up on the Borad's own instructions.

The shock of the mutant seeing himself in the mirror as he really was allowed Peri to break free from his grasp, leaving the large mass of mixed origin cowering from his own reflection.

The Doctors signalled Mykros to activate the Timelash as the Time Lord approached the miserable creature.

'Your reign of terror is over, Borad,' taunted the Doctor, pushing the disfigured mass nearer and nearer to the vortex behind him. 'Nobody loves you, nobody needs you, nobody cares!' With his entire weight and strength, the Doctor rammed the Borad with all the might his body could muster, knocking his opponent off balance and sending him reeling into the Timelash itself.

A discordant yowl faded away as the time corridor consumed the repulsive malformed entity, never to be seen again.

The Doctor didn't have to say a word to Mykros who opened the communication frequency to the descending Bandril ship. He warned the craft to land elsewhere and not use the pad, due to a malfunction. The Bandrils accepted the change of plan and made a new heading for a landing on the flat area on the other side of the Citadel.

'We'll send a welcome party to meet you, Ambassador,' breathed Mykros, very relieved.

Peri rushed to the Doctor, a bright red mark still leaving its impression on her fair complexion around her mouth.

'What was *that*, Doctor?' she asked, rubbing her bruised neck.

'An accident that I hope will never happen again.' The Time Lord turned to Mykros. 'Destroy the clones in the freeze-chambers by blasting a hole in the temperature control units.'

Mykros nodded and left to attend to it. Peri and the Doctor manned the Timelash controls. 'Now to do what I have been itching to do since we first had the misfortune to bump into this infernal corridor.'

'Is it held together by any specific material, Doctor?' The Doctor and Peri turned to see Herbert filling the last page of his notebook. Too engrossed to reply, the Time Lord set the controls on overload, bidding everyone to take cover. A burst of sparks together with a small explosion wrecked the entire box of tricks, making the vortex inoperable.

'I'm sure you'll see it's dismantled, Sezon.'

'It'll be a pleasure, Doctor.'

Peri could sense that it was time to move on. Things seemed tied up quite nicely, and it would be foolish to expect to stay and relax. Her thoughts however had been read for once. The Doctor invited her to enjoy a quiet holiday in the highlands of Scotland.

'But isn't that where you've sent the Borad, Doctor?'

'Same place, different time. I wouldn't worry about

him. He's got a set of flippers and he *does* like water. He'll not harm anyone either.'

Peri's mind was working overtime. 'Surely people will see him?'

The Doctor grinned wryly. 'From time to time...'

'And tell me how you escaped being blasted by the missile, Doctor.'

At one point it seemed as if the Time Lord was going to hold back on his tale, but he eventually enlightened the curious Peri.

'A neat trick. I turned the TARDIS's polarity into a field of negative energy. So much so that the bendalypse warhead was attracted to us, not the planet.'

Peri's question still remained.

'The reason we survived is because Herbert and I time-slipped one hour. When the missile hit, we were simply not there. Since a bendalypse only kills life form, no damage was done on point of impact.'

Herbert was the next to make an announcement. He had decided, after a great deal of thought, that he should like to live on Karfel. Sidetracked by Vena, he wandered off to organise his new life, leaving the Doctor highly amused.

'Will you let him stay, Doctor?' asked Peri.

'The waves of time wash us all clean.'

Peri nudged the Doctor who often infuriated her with his riddles. This time he was quick to explain, producing a calling card from his waistcoat pocket. He showed it to Peri, who could not believe her eyes.

'Herbert dropped this just now, when we dived for cover.'

Peri beamed: 'You mean?'

'The very same. Somehow, I feel that Herbert will be persuaded to return. He's got such an exciting story to tell.'

'I can see how he'll do it too.'

Travelling with the Doctor would inevitably produce the odd surprise and sparkling reward. This time Peri had met someone really special. His card confirmed it.

She looked at it again:

HERBERT GEORGE WELLS.

DOCTOR WHO

0426114558	TERRANCE DICKS **Doctor Who and The Abominable Snowmen**	**£1.35**
0426200373	**Doctor Who and The Android Invasion**	**£1.25**
0426201086	**Doctor Who and The Androids of Tara**	**£1.35**
0426116313	IAN MARTER **Doctor Who and The Ark in Space**	**£1.35**
0426201043	TERRANCE DICKS **Doctor Who and The Armageddon Factor**	**£1.50**
0426112954	**Doctor Who and The Auton Invasion**	**£1.50**
0426116747	**Doctor Who and The Brain of Morbius**	**£1.35**
0426110250	**Doctor Who and The Carnival of Monsters**	**£1.35**
042611471X	MALCOLM HULKE **Doctor Who and The Cave Monsters**	**£1.50**
0426117034	TERRANCE DICKS **Doctor Who and The Claws of Axos**	**£1.35**
042620123X	DAVID FISHER **Doctor Who and The Creature from the Pit**	**£1.35**
0426113160	DAVID WHITAKER **Doctor Who and The Crusaders**	**£1.50**
0426200616	BRIAN HAYLES **Doctor Who and The Curse of Peladon**	**£1.50**
0426114639	GERRY DAVIS **Doctor Who and The Cybermen**	**£1.50**
0426113322	BARRY LETTS **Doctor Who and The Daemons**	**£1.50**

Prices are subject to alteration

DOCTOR WHO

	DAVID WHITAKER	
0426101103	**Doctor Who and The Daleks**	£1.50
042611244X	TERRANCE DICKS **Doctor Who and The Dalek Invasion of Earth**	£1.50
0426103807	**Doctor Who and The Day of the Daleks**	£1.35
042620042X	**Doctor Who – Death to the Daleks**	£1.35
0426119657	**Doctor Who and The Deadly Assassin**	£1.50
0426200969	**Doctor Who and The Destiny of the Daleks**	£1.35
0426108744	MALCOLM HULKE **Doctor Who and The Dinosaur Invasion**	£1.35
0426103726	**Doctor Who and The Doomsday Weapon**	£1.50
0426201464	IAN MARTER **Doctor Who and The Enemy of the World**	£1.50
0426200063	TERRANCE DICKS **Doctor Who and The Face of Evil**	£1.50
0426201507	ANDREW SMITH **Doctor Who – Full Circle**	£1.50
0426112601	TERRANCE DICKS **Doctor Who and The Genesis of the Daleks**	£1.35
0426112792	**Doctor Who and The Giant Robot**	£1.35
0426115430	MALCOLM HULKE **Doctor Who and The Green Death**	£1.35

Prices are subject to alteration

STAR Books are obtainable from many booksellers and newsagents. If you have any difficulty please send purchase price plus postage on the scale below to:

> **Star Cash Sales**
> **P.O. Box 11**
> **Falmouth**
> **Cornwall**
>
> OR
>
> **Star Book Service,**
> **G.P.O. Box 29,**
> **Douglas,**
> **Isle of Man,**
> **British Isles.**

While every effort is made to keep prices low, it is sometimes necessary to increase prices at short notice. Star Books reserve the right to show new retail prices on covers which may differ from those advertised in the text or elsewhere.

Postage and Packing Rate
UK: 55p for the first book, 22p for the second book and 14p for each additional book ordered to a maximum charge of £1.75p. BFPO and EIRE: 55p for the first book, 22p for the second book, 14p per copy for the next 7 books, thereafter 8p per book. Overseas: £1.00p for the first book and 25p per copy for each additional book.

THIS OFFER EXCLUSIVE TO

READERS

**Pin up magnificent full colour posters of
DOCTOR WHO**

**Just send £2.50 for the first poster and £1.25
for each additional poster**

TO: **PUBLICITY DEPARTMENT***
   W. H. ALLEN & CO PLC
   44 HILL STREET
   LONDON W1X 8LB

Cheques, Postal Orders made payable to WH Allen PLC

POSTER 1 ☐   POSTER 2 ☐   POSTER 3 ☐
POSTER 4 ☐   POSTER 5 ☐

Please allow 28 DAYS for delivery.

I enclose £ _____

CHEQUE NO. _____

ACCESS, VISA CARD NO. _____

Name _____

Address _____

_____

_____

***For Australia, New Zealand, USA and Canada apply to distributors
listed on back cover for details and local price list**